Love Comes Back

Ruth Madison

*10% of net royalties from the sale of the Sledge Hockey Team Of Cedar Harbor series will be **donated to https://www.bostonicestorm.org/** Boston's only sled hockey team founded and managed by people with disabilities.*

Titles In The Series

Thawing An Ice Heart
Saving His Soulmate
Hearts Unmasked
Love Comes Back
Holiday Stories

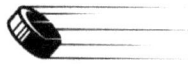

Other Books By Ruth Madison

The Unbroken Novella Series (*Kindle Unlimited)*

The Billionaire's Secretary

Wheely Into You

Stand Alone And Other

The World Between Us

Waiting To Break

Sled Hockey Team Of Cedar Harbor Series

Thawing An Ice Heart

Saving His Soulmate

Hearts Unmasked

Love Comes Back

Get Bonus Content For All Books At:

ruthmadisonbooks.com/bonus

Contents

Fullpage image   VIII

Fullpage image   IX

1. Danny   1

2. Deborah   15

3. Danny   29

4. Deborah   39

5. Danny   50

6. Deborah   60

7. Danny   70

8. Deborah   75

9. Danny   81

10. Deborah   88

11. Danny   104

12. Deborah   115

13. Danny   133

14. Deborah   165

15. Danny   181

16. Deborah   198

17. Danny   213

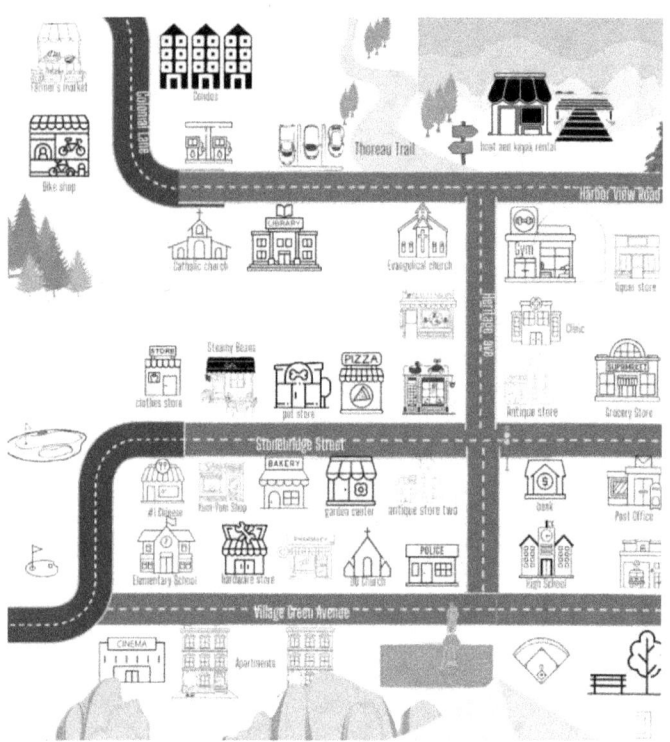

Danny

I push my wheelchair through the front door of The Whispering Pines B&B, noting a few places I can fix up now that it's been a few years since I installed the ramp and flattened the sill and threshold.

There's a new girl at the desk. In a town like Cedar Harbor there's always new people around as patients arrive at Thatcher Memorial Rehab and their families come stay here but I've never seen anyone besides Karen or her wife Susan behind the reception desk.

The girl looks about twelve but that's probably not accurate. I never feel like I'm getting older but the people I encounter in jobs keep looking younger and younger. She asks if I'm looking for a room and gives a quick glance back to the only first-floor room.

"I'm Danny, I'm here to look at the sink leak."

She frowns. "The one in the second-floor bathroom?"

"That's the one."

I don't wait for her to ask all the questions that are currently fighting to get to her lips. I've got my tools in a cross-body belt that looks more like a bandolier than a toolbelt but it stops the screwdriver from digging into my stomach. I push over to the staircase and grab hold of the railing.

Sooner or later everyone around here learns not to question what I'm capable of. I was lucky in one way at least, that my spinal cord injury is incomplete and that gives me enough function to brute force my way through most obstacles. I haul my ass up until I'm standing at the bottom of the stairs, the railing creaking just a little under my full weight. My feet are never flat so I'm on my toes in my work boots.

Very slowly, I pull my way up the stairs, leaning against the wall and using the railing hand over fist to propel me as my feet reluctantly drag up each step one at a time. I don't worry about what it looks like to the gawking teenager below, I've been doing shit like this for thirty-two years. In fact, this is the least outrageous of my stunts.

"Want me to bring that up?" she says and I have to assume she's talking about my chair since I can't risk turning around to look.

"I'll be back for it later," I say, already huffing and out of breath. I'm fifty-three years old and I don't know how long I can keep doing this but if I don't have physical labor, I've got nothing so I always just push through.

On the second floor, I lower myself to the floor and scoot the short distance to the bathroom. The Whispering Pines is such an old-style building that the pipe beneath the tiny sink is exposed, snaking its way along the wall to hook up to the plumbing. Karen's put a bucket under and water is dripping into it at a steady pace. I test the connections but nothing is loose so I pull out my wrench and undo the whole thing, refit the pipe, and tighten it back up again. I lean against the wall while I watch for the drip. Nothing.

"Got you, sucker," I whisper to myself with a mental high-five.

I go back down the stairs on my butt and Karen is waiting at the bottom. The girl from earlier is nowhere to be seen.

"All good?" she says.

"No more leak," I answer. I pull myself back to my wheelchair and can't help a small sigh of relief as my aching butt hits the seat cushion and the effort it takes for me to move is cut by at least half.

"You met Maeve?" she says.

"Is that the new girl at the desk? Yeah."

I'm trying to cut back on the desk hours, let her take over a little."

"Good for you," I say. "Here I thought you were the same level of control freak as me. You ever actually relax, Karen? Or is this just a new flavor of micromanagement?"

She gives me a look, the one that says she's not going to rise to the bait but appreciates the effort. "Oh, I am still very much a control freak," she says. "But Susan keeps threatening to drag me on a cruise if I don't spend less time at the front desk. I'm just trying to avoid being trapped on a boat with my wife and two hundred strangers, is all."

"Sounds like a nightmare." I give her a grin because I know she loves Susan and wouldn't have it any other way.

"You want to stay for dinner?" Karen asks. "Susan's making tortellini."

"I gotta get over to hockey practice," I say, glad to have an excuse. I like the ladies and all but I prefer my quiet and simple dinners at home. Plus Karen has that worried look on her face that tells me dinner will be an excuse to probe about my personal life. She pushes off from the wall and goes into host mode again, all business. "You want me to send you off with something? A sandwich, maybe?"

"If you've got that tuna salad, I wouldn't say no."

She grins, "Always do."

While I wait, I look at the landscape paintings along the hallway towards the kitchen. They are all different artists' depictions of the local area. Right in front of me there's an old walnut grandfather clock that's never once kept the right time even when Karen winds it. I can hear the sound of the ocean through the open window by the staircase, and the way it blends with the distant clang of the church bell. It's almost poetic, if you're in the mood.

"Say hi to Murph for me," Karen says as she hands me a paper baggie.

I push out the front door into the chill air that bristles my nose hairs. No snow yet this year but the mornings have been frosty. The gym is just a mile down the road; nothing in Cedar Harbor is too far, but I have hockey equipment in the truck so I'll still drive. I hold onto the side to stand up, then heave the wheelchair into the truck bed and lean against the side to get to the driver's door.

I get in and turn off the defroster. It did its work this morning and now I can just put on the regular heat. Even though I have function in my legs, it's not strong enough or consistent enough for driving so I use hand controls that I installed myself. I find there's nothing more satisfying than solving a problem with your own two hands.

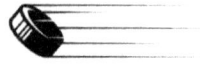

At the rec center, the ice rink is all the way at the back so I put my gym bag on my lap and wheel past the front desk and the various other rooms with machines, free weights, cardio, and more. The locker room is situated between the pool and the rink so it always smells of chlorine, soap, and sweat.

Our little team is growing. We're up to five players now and I was one of the first three. It was actually Karen who told me about it. I hadn't done team sports since high school and it's been fun to get back into it even though we haven't played any games yet. I usually arrive early because some of the other guys need help with their gear.

Murph founded the team and he used to be a paralympic-level pro sled hockey player so he's good unless someone put something away on a high shelf. Robbie plays more sports than I can count but he doesn't have strength in his hands and his fingers aren't very mobile so me or Murph tighten his straps. Then there's Mark, a teen with CP, and he needs the most help. He's a sweet kid and being on the team seems to be helping bring him out of his shell. I teach shop classes to kids his age. Finally there's Jack who is not only new to the wheeler life, but I don't think he's ever played a sport in his life. He's the kind of guy who worries about his hair getting messed up. He hasn't yet gotten used to not relying on his legs but he'll get speedier as time goes on.

Murph is the first to arrive after me. Today his t-shirt says *I'm kind of a big dill*. Can always count on him for the shirt puns. He doesn't talk much so he provides entertainment through his fashion choices.

"How's it going?" I ask.

"Good." He's quick to slide his light-weight protective shorts over the small amount of leg he has left on each side and catches all the way up to me so we're both finished putting on our gear at the same time.

Once everyone arrives and gets changed, we all wheel out to the rink to get into our sleds. The first few practices Mark's mom stayed and helped with his but over time she started trusting that I could help him transfer. The sleds are all custom to our needs but getting them used up all of our budget for the year so I know we'll be talking fundraising before too long.

My arms burn as I dig the metal picks of my sticks into the ice, propelling myself forward. Sweat drips into my eyes. The scrape of metal on ice fills the rink as we race from end to end, our sleds hissing across the surface. I pivot to face Robbie, flipping my right stick around to catch the puck he fires my way. It smacks against the blade with a satisfying thwack. Jack fumbles his stick transition, the puck skittering away as he curses under his breath.

Later, I guard the net while Mark tries to score, his face tight with concentration. His sled wobbles slightly as he approaches. Jack slams into the boards with a hollow thud, the collision rattling through the rink.

Murph's voice echoes across the ice. "Jack, pay attention to who's around you, including the wall."

"Alright, we're running the Canadian box drill," Murph calls. "Pairs of two, one on offense, one on D, cycle through, keep it fast. No contact, Jack, but that doesn't mean you can coast. Understood?"

Jack raises a hand, deadpan. "Define 'no contact' for me?"

Murph narrows his eyes. "If your mother would sue me, it's contact."

"Roger that," Jack says. If he's embarrassed, he doesn't show it.

We line up at the blue line. Robbie and I take the first run. He's fast, even for a guy with no triceps, and his upper body is pure torque from years of propelling a manual. We jockey for position, sticks clattering, and he jukes left, then right, then tries to slip past with a feint. I block him with a shoulder, spin, and chase him down to the net, where he slaps a puck straight in past Murph, who is acting as goalie.

Next up is Mark and Jack. Mark's nervous at first, but once he's got the puck, he's single-minded. Jack tries to sweep him, but Mark just plows forward, all elbows and determination, and actually scores. The rest of us bang sticks on the ice for him. Murph watches, impassive, but I can tell he's impressed.

The drill goes on like this for twenty minutes. By the end, everyone's sweating, even in the cold. I love this part, the exhaustion that comes from moving fast and hitting hard, the way it drowns out everything else.

But then Mark pulls up and waves a hand. "Um, something's loose," he says. His left bracket is rattling, the sled wobbling with each push.

"Let me look," I say, steering over. He stops and waits, trusting, while I dig in the pouch on my hip for the Allen wrench. I tuck the end of my sled under his frame to hold it steady, then work the wrench into the bracket, tightening until the metal squeaks. It's the same way I'd fix a faucet, methodical, precise.

"There," I say. "Should be good."

Mark grins, relief flooding his face. "Thanks, Danny."

"Anytime," I say, and mean it. I shove back into the lineup, glad for something I can fix.

We finish the drill and Murph calls us in. He waits for everyone to settle before he starts.

"You looked better tonight," he says, resting an arm across the front of his sled. "If we keep this up, maybe we won't embarrass ourselves when we finally get to a real game."

Robbie whoops, "That's the spirit, Coach!"

Jack raises a hand again. "Question: if we do embarrass ourselves, can we claim it's for charity?"

Murph levels a look at him. "We are the charity, Jack."

Robbie's laughing so hard he almost falls out of his sled.

Murph waits for the noise to die down. "Alright. Off the ice, stretch, and then hit the showers."

I notice from the corner of my eye that the girlfriends have arrived. Love is in the air around Cedar Harbor. People are pairing up all over the place. Some of them don't surprise me. Robbie's been pining for Samantha for a long time and earlier this year we all worked together to get her out of a bad situation. Murph and Carly are both leaders and they complement each other well. But Becca and Jack I really don't get. He's all corporate speak and slick packaging while she's earnest and direct. Then again, what do I know about love? I haven't dated in years and my track record back then sucked anyway.

Carly, Samantha, and Becca watch the last few minutes of our practice then we all get off the ice and back into our wheelchairs. Murph, me, and the girls get the sleds put away.

"Do you want to join us for dinner?" Sam asks me, knowing that Mark's mom always picks him up promptly to go home and do homework.

"No thanks," I say. What wheel would I be if I went out to dinner with three couples that all include one wheelchair user? Thirteenth, fourteenth, fifteenth, and sixteenth I guess.

"Meet you out front," Carly says to Murph. He has his helmet on his lap so she leans over to kiss his sweaty forehead before all the guys head back into the locker room to change.

Afterwards, Mark and I sit side by side outside the gym in the chilly air and watch the couples leaving for dinner together.

"What's in the water lately?" I say, shaking my head.

"Whatever it is, I want some," he says with such complete sincerity it breaks my heart a little.

I clap him on the shoulder. "Me too, kid."

Then his mother's van pulls up and I am free to finally return home after another long day. Despite my daily work in the community, I am an introvert at heart and my favorite time is my evenings at home.

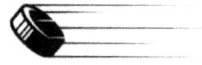

I don't live in Cedar Harbor even though most of my business is there. I live a couple towns away where I grew up. I'm Massachusetts born and bred and I've never lived anywhere else. In fact, a few years ago I moved back into the house I lived in with my dad in high school. I pull my truck into the driveway and grab my wheelchair from the back. The house is a quaint little cape coder and I've made a number of modifications for accessibility but the core of it remains the same. There's a long, low-grade wooden ramp that extends from the driveway directly to the front door. There's no porch on the house and only three brick steps up, which I can technically manage, but when renovating the house to make it my own I decided to make it completely ideal for me. The ramp being as long as it is means I also don't have to wheel over grass or the concrete path and I can easily snow blow it off in the winter.

There's a staircase in front of me the moment I roll in, but I haven't used it in years. The rooms upstairs aren't that useful anyway. The ceiling is low and slopes down dramatically. It's basically just storage up there.

At home I mostly use a walker. In the entrance I grip the handles and pull myself up out of the wheelchair. I keep my boots on for stability. I limp heavily to the kitchen leaning on the walker. Because my injury is incomplete, I have random muscles that are paralyzed and others that aren't. One knee doesn't straighten all the way, which makes my gait very uneven, more a lurch than a walk.

I put a frozen dinner in the microwave. Despite the offer for a home-cooked meal and the offer for a restaurant meal tonight, I'll take the frozen one because it comes with being able to fully relax. Once it's done, I put it on the seat of the walker and carry it that way to the living room.

With a satisfied sigh, I sink down into my recliner, put the dinner on a tray table, and turn on the TV.

This is perfection. A full day's work, some exercise with the guys, and a quiet evening at home. It's not the life I once envisioned for myself but I'm happy with it. And there's a real benefit to no one else being here to judge my taste in TV, I think, as I turn on The Real Housewives. I don't even care which city. There's nothing better than watching catty drama with people whose lives are a million worlds away from yours.

Finally I take my achy bones to bed. My calves are on fire. Probably from the stair climbing today. I press my fingers into the muscles, massaging as best I can. I finish my evening routine (stretches, medication) then lay back in bed, propping my head against the lumpy wedge pillow that's supposed to keep my spine aligned. The sheets are cold, but in a pleasant way—sharp enough to jolt me out of thinking about my body for a second and focus on the here and now. I check my phone out of habit, see a few texts from Karen but nothing urgent. No missed calls. The world is content to leave me alone for the night, and I'm grateful.

My eyelids grow heavy, and the pain in my legs fades to background static. It's always at this moment, right as I'm drifting off, that my mind starts to wander. Not to work or hockey or the endless list of repairs Cedar Harbor needs, but to Deb. She was my first love, and honestly still the only real one. I picture her, older now but still with that sly smile, living the life she always wanted. I hope the man she left me for has made her happy and given her everything I couldn't.

Deborah

I grip the steering wheel tighter as we pass the old Dunkin' Donuts that's now a vape shop. My GPS keeps recalculating because I think I know better and it turns out, I don't. Then suddenly there's the oak tree with the lightning scar, unchanged after thirty years. My breath catches.

"Mom?" Alana's voice pulls me back. "Are we going to pass the school you went to?"

"Not today," I say, blinking hard.

I should be grateful I have a teenage daughter who still speaks to me but as we drive into Massachusetts, I wish she would stop with all the questions. She's curious about this place and my history here but I don't even have the words to explain how it feels to return after thirty-two years away.

Her phone chimes with the special tone she set for my mother. "Bubbe wants to know why we aren't going straight to their place."

I inhale slowly through my nose. Three missed calls already. The divorce papers still warm in my glove compartment. "Tell her I'll call her in the morning."

Alana types, then sighs. "She sent back just a question mark. Seems like a waste of money when we can stay at Bubbe and Zayda's for free."

Free isn't exactly what I'd call it but I don't say anything. We drive past the turnoff to my parents' neighborhood without comment. I notice the setting sun illuminating my bare ring finger.

We turn onto the main drag of Cedar Harbor, Massachusetts, and she lets out a theatrical groan. "Mom, did you Google 'quaint New England' and just click the first result?"

Alana's got her phone out, filming the streetscape for what I can only assume is a TikTok she'll caption "witness protection, but make it cozy." She pans past a man in a wheelchair hauling a duffel up the ramp to the ice rink, then zooms in on a battered Subaru with its hood up. "Is everyone here seventy-five and named after a president?"

"Don't be ageist," I say, and she cackles.

We reach the turn off Stonebridge Street onto Cottage Grove Ave, where the Whispering Pines B&B sits in full Victorian splendor: three stories, gables and gingerbread trim, porch swing creaking in the wind. The sign out front is hand-carved, the paint a little chipped. I pull into the gravel driveway and stare up at the house.

Alana doesn't wait for me to cut the engine. She pops the trunk, slings her backpack over one shoulder and marches up the front steps. I linger, staring at the windows. There's a curtain twitch upstairs—a ghost, or more likely Karen, peeking to see if the city people have arrived. The air smells like woodsmoke and salt. A couple gulls wheel overhead, screaming at each other with the same energy as every holiday dinner we ever had.

I'm halfway to the porch when the front door bursts open and Karen barrels out. She hasn't changed at all: same flannel, same jeans, hair pulled back in a stubby ponytail, a posture that says she could wrestle a bear and win, if only because the bear would get tired first.

"Debbie Klein, you son of a bitch," she yells, and envelops me in a hug so tight my spine pops. "You made it!" She smells like fresh bread and dryer sheets, her hands rough from years of work. I let myself be squeezed and it feels nice.

"Hey, Karen," I say, muffled by her shoulder.

She holds me at arm's length and looks me up and down. "Still allergic to Massachusetts, or did the doctors finally find you a cure?"

Alana snorts behind me. "She's trying out exposure therapy. So far it's mostly hives."

Karen winks at her. "Smart kid. I always said you'd get all your brains from your mom."

"Not what Dad says," Alana mutters, but she's grinning.

Karen shoulders my suitcase and gestures us inside. "C'mon, c'mon, you look like you need a drink and a nap, in either order. Susan made apple cider, and she's been fussing all morning about getting the room just right. I told her you'd sleep on a cement floor if it meant you could close your eyes for ten hours, but she insisted on mints and color-coordinated towels."

The foyer is a riot of old pine and battered rugs. There's a coat rack by the door and a row of mismatched slippers for guests, which Alana inspects with the skepticism of a TSA agent. The floorboards creak with every step, and the air inside is warm, full of yeast and cinnamon.

Karen leads us to the parlor, where a fire snaps in the grate and a table is laid out with cookies, sliced cheddar, and an actual pitcher of cider. There are mismatched mugs stacked at one end, and a vase of holly branches at the other.

Alana flops onto the loveseat and pulls out her phone again, thumbs flying.

"Don't mind her," I say, but Karen just grins. "She's probably posting your cookie platter to Instagram."

"Hope she gets my good side," Karen says, dropping my suitcase at the bottom of the stairs and pouring me a mug of cider. "So," she says, lowering her voice, "how're you holding up?"

I take the mug and cradle it in both hands, letting the steam fog my glasses. "We're here," I say, which isn't an answer, but Karen takes it as one. She glances at Alana and I'm grateful she realizes I don't want to fall apart in front of the daughter I just forced to move with me.

Karen settles onto the edge of the ottoman, knees apart, elbows on thighs, a pose that's more coach than innkeeper. "You look better than I expected, honestly. When I heard about the split, I thought you'd show up shaved bald and wearing tie-dye."

"Give me a week," I say, managing a weak laugh. "I haven't even unpacked the crisis wardrobe yet."

Karen shakes her head, fond and a little pitying. "Listen, you need anything—tools, paint, a sledgehammer—just say the word. We can fix anything around here except the

TV reception, and even that's only because Susan keeps buying off-brand antennas."

Susan appears in the doorway right on cue, holding a tray with more cookies. She's smaller than I remember, softer around the edges, with a streak of silver in her hair that wasn't there last time. She's wearing a long, flowy cardigan that brushes the backs of her hands, and her smile is the kind that makes you feel like you just came in from a blizzard.

"Hi, Deborah," she says, using the full name, like always. "You made good time! And this must be Alana."

Alana glances up and manages a polite "Hi."

"I hope you're hungry," Susan says. "Dinner will be done soon. Did you have any trouble finding the place?"

"None," I say. "The sign's crooked, though."

Karen groans. "The windstorm last year knocked it sideways. I was going to fix it, but the guests said it had 'character.'"

"It does," I say, and I mean it.

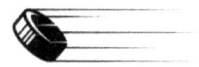

I haven't felt this relaxed in a long time. Maybe years. The thought drifts lazily through my mind, unbidden, like a leaf floating down a slow-moving stream. My shoulders, which always seem to carry the weight of some unseen burden, have finally loosened, dropping from their usual defensive hunch. I lean back in the dining room seat. The rich scent of butter and garlic lingers in the air, mingling with the faint citrus tang of whatever cleaning spray Susan must have used earlier. It's a smell that feels like home—warm, inviting, and lived-in—the kind of place that doesn't demand perfection but offers solace instead.

Across the room, Karen is in her element, weaving a tale with her usual flair for embellishment. Her hands carve through the air as she speaks, punctuating each sentence with exaggerated gestures that make Alana laugh so hard she almost spills her water. "And then," Karen says, dragging the words out as if savoring the suspense, "she stands up on the table—no, I swear to God, *a cafeteria table*—and shouts, 'If you can't beat 'em, join 'em!'" She pauses for dramatic effect, her grin widening as she turns to me. "Tell me I'm lying, Deb."

I groan, covering my face with both hands, though the smile tugging at my lips gives me away. "You're not lying," I admit through my fingers, my voice muffled but tinged with laughter. "But you're leaving out the part where you dared me to do it in the first place."

Karen gasps in mock indignation, clutching her chest like I've just accused her of high treason. "I would *never*! I was an innocent bystander, just as shocked as everyone else."

"Please," I shoot back, lowering my hands to reveal an arched eyebrow. "You practically handed me a megaphone."

Alana, perched cross-legged on the formal chair like she's settling in for a performance, shakes her head in disbelief. Her dark eyes dance with amusement as she looks between us. "You really did that? Stood on a cafeteria table? I can't even picture it."

"Oh, it happened," Karen cuts in before I can answer, her voice dripping with faux solemnity. "It was like watching a train wreck, horrifying but impossible to look away from."

"Thanks for that," I say dryly, though I can't help laughing. The sound feels strange in my chest—light and unrestrained, like it hasn't been used in far too long.

Susan chooses that moment to emerge from the kitchen, carrying a platter of roasted chicken and vegetables that glistens under the warm overhead lights. She sets it on the table with a flourish, her smile soft but proud. "Dinner is served," she announces, wiping her hands on a dishtowel before tossing it over her shoulder.

The sight of the meal stirs something deep in me, an ache I didn't realize was there until now. It's not just hunger, though my stomach growls in anticipation; it's the care behind it, the thoughtfulness of someone taking the time to cook for me. For all of us. It's been a long time since I wasn't the one soley responsible for making sure every person in the house got fed. The chicken is golden and crisp, surrounded by a rainbow of carrots, parsnips, and potatoes that look like they've been kissed by herbs and olive oil.

"This looks amazing," I say, my voice quieter now, almost reverent. I glance at Susan, who waves off the compliment with an easy shrug.

"Just something simple," she says, though there's a small blush creeping up her neck.

As we gather around the table, passing plates and pouring wine, I feel an unfamiliar but welcome sensation settle over me: peace. The kind that doesn't demand anything of me. The kind that lets me just be. I catch myself exhaling deeply, as if my body is finally remembering how to breathe properly. It's like I've been holding my breath for years.

As we clink glasses and dig into the meal, laughter fills the room again: Karen launching into another wild story, Alana egging her on, Susan chuckling quietly at their antics. I find myself watching them, soaking it all in like sunlight after a long winter.

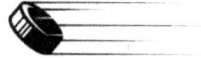

Hours later, the hush of midnight presses against the windows. I sit on the edge of the bed, watching oak and pine silhouettes sway beyond the sheer curtains. Their limbs murmur against one another, a soft hiss that gives this place its name. Alana's breathing rises and falls beside me, even and oblivious. My heart, however, is jittery as sparks. After a moment, I slip into fuzzy slippers, pull the plush cream robe around my shoulders, and tiptoe into the hallway, the floorboards groaning beneath me.

There's light downstairs and I make my way in that direction, expecting to hear a clatter of dishes going into the dishwasher but instead there's a gentle clink of crystal drifting in from the glassed-in side porch. An amber lamp glows behind lace curtains. Through the double doors, Karen and Susan lounge on a wicker daybed strewn with crocheted pillows and a knit throw.

Susan sees me first and her face lights up in a bright smile. "Join us," she says, extending a fresh crystal goblet.

I take the glass, its stem cool under my fingers, and sink into a papasan chair that rocks softly.

Karen fixes me with a long look. Now that my daughter isn't here she says, "How are you doing really?"

I swallow against the tightness in my throat. "I don't know, I'm...adrift," I admit, voice low. "I thought I'd done everything right: married at the right time, bought the right house, raised a daughter who sleeps like an angel. But now I feel like I burned my life down and I can't even name why. I followed every rule, ticked every box. Why do I feel like this?"

Deep down I know the answer. I chose practicality over love. I thought love was the least important thing. I thought love could be planted and nurtured so if you didn't have it, you could still grow it.

I chose what seemed like security and a promising future instead of love. How would things be different if I made the opposite choice? Maybe it was inevitable that things would fall apart, no matter which way I went. But I don't really believe that. I think my family was wrong. I think my community was wrong. I think I had the kind of love that could overcome and I threw it away.

Susan leans forward, folding her hands over her knee. "Practicality often wears the cloak of wisdom," she says softly. "I chased security when I was your age—steady job, neat lawn, all the trappings. But security isn't always happy. I was divorced when I met Karen."

"You were? Would it be terrible for me to ask...did you have a good reason?"

She chuckles a little. "For anyone else I would say that's private and not answer. But I'll be honest tonight." Susan lifts her glass in a quiet toast. "We convince ourselves that to break a vow we need a reason vast enough for everyone to understand. No matter how unhappy we are, the line is always far away. The reason is never big enough. So we cling to discomfort for years, waiting for a sign. Until one day we realize happiness isn't optional, it's essential. And you—and your partner—deserve someone who chooses you, without hesitation."

Karen's hand finds Susan's knee, warm and reassuring. They exchange a look rich with shared storms and laughter.

I press my palm over my wineglass, the room shrinking to that single table, the lamp's glow, the pulse of my heart. "That's a lot to process on one glass of wine after a long drive," I whisper.

Susan smiles at me. "Give it time, it will all start to make sense."

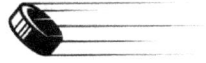

Thankfully, Alana is the sort of sleeper who could nap through a tornado, so when I slip back into bed beside her, she only snuffles a little, rolling to face the window without ever really surfacing. I tuck the covers up under her chin, then lie flat on my back and stare at the ceiling. I want to believe that sleep will come, but my head is a carousel of everything—the things I said, the things I didn't.

After a few useless minutes of counting backwards from a hundred, I swipe my phone from the nightstand and plug in an earpiece. With the screen dimmed low, I queue up a Real Housewives episode (season 8, Orange County, the only one worth rewatching) and let the savage pettiness of reality television drown out my thoughts. Alana always teases me about these shows, but there's something hypnotic about women with too much money and not nearly enough perspective.

Finally I set my phone to Do Not Disturb and close my eyes. Somewhere in the dark, I dream about standing in an empty house, every cabinet and closet thrown open, every drawer emptied onto the floor. I am looking for something irreplaceable, but I wake up before I can find it.

The next morning, my phone buzzes against the head-board and I squint blearily at the screen: Mom calling at 7:21 a.m., right on schedule.

Danny

Thatcher Memorial Rehabilitation Center is visible from every point in Cedar Harbor, a brick-and-glass beacon of medical determination. From a distance, it looks almost like a school, and in a way, that's what it is. Thatcher teaches people how to re-enter the world after their bodies and sense of self have been ground up and spit back out by fate. Every hallway here is a lesson in learning to live with less, or with different, or with new. The place smells of antiseptic and linoleum, but under that is something sweeter, like hope trying to hide itself from predators.

When I pull up in my truck, the lot is half-full, mostly staff and a parade of battered family cars. There's a cluster of construction workers too, who are finishing an expansion on the east wing. I park in my usual spot, which is half a space wider than normal. Almost half the spaces in the lot are accessible ones. Thatcher was one of the first in the state to go above and beyond ADA regs, a point of pride for Dr. Wilson and every patient who's ever come through the doors.

Inside, Thatcher is busy but not chaotic. The lobby has been recently tiled, the grout still blindingly pale. Half the walls are glass and fill the space with honest natural light. At the front desk, Monica waves me past without looking up from her phone, her uncanny ability to multi-task an entire building's worth of appointments and gossip on full display.

Today, my job is to refresh the paint on the right side of the main lobby, which has spent the past six months getting scuffed by wheelchairs, walkers, and the occasional projectile IV stand. The prep crew already moved most of the furniture and laid out drop cloths. I add a few of my own, then start the relay of moving supplies from my truck one at a time on my lap. A few more tarps, tape to hold them down so I can wheel over without them bunching up, rollers and paintbrushes with extension poles, trays, and finally the paint. It's called "Driftwood," a gentle gray that's supposed to evoke comfort, neutrality, and nobility.

Personally, I think it looks like a cloud on a dirty day, but I'm not the one who picks the color palette.

Once all the supplies are laid out around the floor of the lobby, it's quick to get started. I don't use painters tape because I can't reach high enough to put it on. I'm just extra careful with the roller. It requires concentration, but it's possible .

I'm just hitting my stride when I feel the air shift behind me. It's not a draft—it's the sense of someone standing close, someone who owns the space and doesn't need to say a word to prove it.

"You taking care of yourself?" comes the voice, gravelly and precise, as familiar to me as my own pulse.

I set down the roller and turn to face Dr. Rita Wilson, the unchallenged queen of Thatcher Memorial. Her hair is a mass of gray and black curls, her frame is wiry, and her grin is sharp as ever. She wears the same white lab coat she's had for decades, the pockets heavy with pens and notepads and, for some reason, ancient throat lozenges. I've known her since I was eighteen and didn't believe in chronic pain or consequences. She wrote the prescription for every one of my painkillers in those early months after my injury, signed off on my first set of hand controls, and called me a "fucking idiot" when I wrecked my first car. Naturally, I adore her.

I grin. "Live fast, die young?"

She snorts and says, "Too late for that, Dan. You're about three decades behind schedule."

"Guess I'll have to settle for moderately paced and well-preserved."

"Promise me you aren't working yourself into an early grave," she says before leaving me to it, her gait athletic and unapologetic, her shoes echoing so loudly everyone in the building knows where she is.

I finish the first coat and use the break while it dries to wander into the cafeteria, which is one part lunchroom and one part social club for the broken-bodied and their minders. I grab a coffee and a day-old muffin, then scan the room for familiar faces. There are plenty—this place is like a second home to anyone who's ever needed a tune-up on their brace or a pep talk from someone who gets it.

At a corner table, I spot Robbie, who's been coming here since high school. He waves me over with a forkful of eggs and says, "Hey, it's Mr. Do-It-All. They got you painting again?"

"Somebody's gotta keep up with your reckless abandon," I say, and we spend five minutes swapping war stories about the week. Robbie's the kind of guy who tries every adaptive sport at least once, and he's got the orthopedic hardware to prove it. Last month it was skiing. The month before, he crashed a handcycle into a mailbox. Both times, he ended up with more confidence and less skin.

I finish my muffin, check my schedule, and head back to the lobby.

The second coat goes on easier than the first, and by two o'clock I'm touching up the corners with a fine brush, listening to the soundtrack of nurses gossiping and the distant whirr of power chairs in the hallway. I catch Dr. Wilson watching me from the other side of the glass, her arms crossed and her expression somewhere between pleased and skeptical. Sometimes she thinks it's great for the patients to see me doing my work as someone like them with a spinal cord injury. Other times she threatens to stick a "Do Not Try This At Home" disclaimer sticker to my back.

It's the same look she had when I came back to Thatcher as a certified handyman. She watched over me doing rehab here, then I did what no one expected and went to trade school. You should have seen the looks my first day there. Conversations stopped as I passed. I heard a few whispers like, "Can we officially say that political correctness has gone too far?" and "Diversity hiring is starting younger and younger." But when I managed to install a light fixture in a vaulted ceiling, my teachers started taking me seriously.

My classmates called me a daredevil but really I just didn't have a choice. My grades weren't good enough for college, my family didn't have money, at that point my dad was fading. The worst that could happen if I failed was death and that was going to be my fate if I didn't do it too. So I just kept going.

When I finish the second coat of paint, I wheel back and take a long look at the wall. It's nothing special, just a few square yards of driftwood gray, but it's the backdrop to every reunion and every hard conversation in this place. I hope it holds up.

Packing up, I do a victory lap through the wings, checking on a couple small repairs I'd meant to tackle—loose drawer in the OT room, a sticky sliding door in the east stairwell. Everywhere I go, someone calls out my name, and I can't help but feel a sense of ownership. Not of the building itself, but of the stories embedded in these walls.

I load my old blue pickup like it's a clown car: drop cloths, empty coffee cups, half-used energy bars, the mishmash of a real working man's backseat. I could call it a day, but I promised Karen I'd stop by The Whispering Pines before heading home.

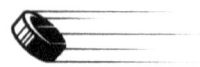

Now that I'm here, I'm starting to suspect it was a ruse.

"You want me to check the breaker box?"

"Uh huh," she says, her voice wavering.

I raise an eyebrow. "You're a terrible liar, you know that?"

"That obvious?" She wipes her hands on her apron and leans in, voice lowering. "Okay, okay. I wasn't totally straight with you."

"Try not to shock me," I say, fighting a smile.

"I have this friend. I want you to take her out on a date."

"Karen!"

"It's perfect. She's an old friend, recently divorced and new in town. You and her both need to get out there."

"Who says I need to get out there?"

"I do?" she tries and I roll my eyes.

"Oh come on, Danny, it will be a nice evening and you'll help make her feel connected to the community."

"You aren't going to let this go, are you?"

Karen grins. She doesn't have to answer, she knows she's won. A night out won't be so bad. The constant rotation of tv dinners can't be good for me. So I'll meet this woman and laugh with her about how relentless Karen can be.

"Fine. I'll do it. But if this is another set-up where she actually just needs her gutters cleaned, I'm billing you double."

Karen laughs. "Deal. I'll arrange everything. Her name's Deborah."

A jolt goes through me like someone tapping a tuning fork against my ribcage. Even after all these years, the name hits different. It takes me back to senior year. Debbie Cohen with her chestnut hair and that crooked smile that made my knees weak. I remember walking down the hallway in my Metallica t-shirt, spotting her at her locker, books clutched to her chest.

"Yo, Danny-boy!" Mike Tavares had shouted from across the hall. "Your other half is waiting!"

I'd rolled my eyes but couldn't hide my grin. The whole school knew us as "Danny and Debbie," like we were some package deal you couldn't separate. I secretly loved it. I never felt like part of a team before. Usually it was just me and my dad, doing our best to get by.

"You heading to the bonfire tonight?" Debbie had asked when I reached her, pushing up on her tiptoes to kiss my cheek.

"Only if you are," I'd answered, slipping my arm around her waist.

Joey Martinez had passed by, making exaggerated kissing noises. "Danny and Debbie sitting in a tree!"

"Real mature, Joey," Debbie had called after him, but she was laughing.

We were from different worlds. Me, the shop class kid from the run-down cape on Bradlock Lane. Dad working double shifts at the warehouse while I fixed everything that broke at home. And Debbie, honor student with the lawyer dad and the house on the hill with the perfect lawn.

"My parents think I should be dating Joel Klein," she'd confided one night as we sat on the edge of the old train overpass bridge, staring at stars.

"That lame ass?" I'd snorted. "Guy can't even change a tire."

She'd laughed, laying her head on my shoulder. "I don't care that you can change a tire. I just love you."

It was so simple then. Her hand in mine, our names linked together like they were meant to be that way. Danny and Debbie. Debbie and Danny.

I say goodnight to Karen and Susan and drive home through the purple dusk in silence, not even listening to the radio.

That night my dreams are pierced by different views and angles of dark asphalt, shiny from rain, the droplets so small they're invisible in the night, but the pavement is still slick and glowing from it. The texture of the asphalt becomes grainier as I seem to get closer and closer to it, perhaps about to be swallowed in the deep black. Then I am being swallowed by it, instead of a hard surface it's turned into a deep black pool of sludge. Sound stops as the sludge fills my ears and there's nothing but total darkness all around me.

I wake up in the middle of the night with nerve pain cinching up and down my legs. I grit my teeth while I wait for it to settle down. Outside the window is dark and I have the uncomfortable feeling that the past is coming for me.

Deborah

When I get out of the car I first wonder if I got the directions wrong. I turn around in a circle. None of the houses in sight look anything like what the realtor and I talked about. All around me are what can only be described as McMansions with perfectly manicured lawns. I told the realtor that I wanted a small place with lots of charm, the quirkier the better. I wonder how I could have gone to the wrong place and how late I'm going to be for the appointment but then I see the realtor striding towards me with a bright smile.

"Deborah! Great to meet you in person. I'm Allison."

I shake the offered hand. "Sorry, Allison, I'm confused. Where is the house we talked about?"

Her eyes open wide for a second and a flush spreads across her neck. "I thought...I mean, didn't your mother tell you?"

Uh oh. What does my mother have to do with this? "No, she didn't tell me anything."

"She called yesterday. She told me that she was helping you out with the house and that you had agreed you needed something a bit bigger. Is that not accurate?"

I don't want to put this woman in the middle or make her feel awkward just because my mom has never heard of the word "boundaries."

"Not exactly," I answer. "I'm still interested in smaller places. It's just me and my daughter. I'll clear things up with my mother but you can go ahead and just schedule the tours that I requested."

"Totally understood," Allison says, shuffling through papers that have appeared in her hands. "Since we're here, do you want to take a look?" She gestures towards the ugliest house on the street.

"No, that's okay. Let's reschedule."

On my drive back to The Whispering Pines I call my mom.

"Can you explain to me why my realtor told me that you are choosing the houses now?"

"You don't need to be snippy."

"I'm not being snippy," I say, trying to keep my voice steady. "I'm just surprised that you went behind my back."

"Behind your back?" My mother's voice rises an octave. "I was helping you! Do you know what kind of neighborhood that tiny cottage was in? The schools are terrible."

I grip the steering wheel tighter, counting to three in my head before responding. "Mom, I researched the schools. They're perfectly fine."

"Fine isn't good enough for Alana," she snaps. "After everything that poor girl has been through with the divorce, don't you think she deserves the best? Those big houses have pools, Deborah. Think about how much she'd love having friends over to swim."

I pull into the parking lot of The Whispering Pines and shut off the engine, staying in the car to finish this conversation without an audience. "Alana doesn't need a pool. She needs stability and happiness, which I can provide in a small, manageable house that I can actually afford."

"We told you we'd help with the down payment."

"I don't want your help," I say, more forcefully than intended. "I don't want strings attached to where I live."

There's silence on the other end, and I know I've hurt her feelings. But I'm tired of this—tired of having my choices questioned, of being treated like I can't make decisions for my own life.

"Strings?" she finally says, her voice quiet. "Is that what you think of our generosity? Strings?"

I sigh. "That's not what I meant. But Mom, this is my life. Mine and Alana's. I get to decide what's best for us, not you and Dad."

"We just want what's best for our granddaughter."

"So do I," I say softly. "But what's best isn't always the biggest or most expensive option. I want a home I can manage on my own. Something with character that feels like us."

"Character is just a fancy word for 'needs work,'" my mother mutters.

Despite everything, I laugh. "Maybe. But it's still my choice."

"Fine," she says after a moment, though her tone makes it clear it's anything but. "I'll call your realtor back and tell her there was a misunderstanding."

"Thank you," I say, relief washing over me. "I appreciate that."

"Will you at least come to dinner tomorrow? Your father misses you both."

The guilt trip is so expected I almost smile. "We'll come to dinner. But please, Mom, no more house talk unless I bring it up first. Deal?"

She sighs dramatically. "Deal."

I end the call and rest my forehead against the steering wheel for a moment. Standing up to my mother has never been easy, but since the divorce, it's become necessary. For fifty-three years I've lived the life others expected of me. Now, I'm determined to build something that's me before it's too late.

I can't help worrying, though, if I am right about what's best for my daughter. Speaking with certainty is the only way to deal with my mother, I can't let her know that she has pierced through my armor a little bit.

There are things about my childhood that I don't want for Alana but of course I don't want her to have less than what I had. We all want the best for our kids and to give them more than what we had. What if choosing the cozy house of my dreams really does mean that I'm giving her less and depriving her of the life she could have. It's an impossible thought process. Children are so complicated. There's no way to fully know what is going to help them or harm them when it comes to things like this. But what if my mother is right? What if I'm being selfish choosing a smaller home when Alana could have more? I need to get some outside perspective on this.

Thankfully, Alana is now in school. Even though we don't have a permanent address yet, the Cedar Harbor high school is letting her attend there until it's all sorted out.

I step out of the car, taking a deep breath of the pine-scented air. The Whispering Pines looks like a haven right now with its welcoming porch and weathered shingles.

Karen is at the front desk when I enter, organizing brochures for local attractions. She looks up with a smile that quickly fades when she sees my expression.

"Rough day?" she asks, setting down her stack of papers.

"You could say that." I collapse into one of the armchairs by the grandfather clock. "My mother called my realtor behind my back and tried to get me to look at McMansions instead of the cottage I wanted."

Karen's eyebrows shoot up. "Wow. That's...impressive boundary-crossing, even for a Jewish mother."

I laugh despite myself. "She thinks I'm depriving Alana of the best schools and a swimming pool."

Karen comes around the desk and sits in the chair opposite me. "And what do you think?"

"I think..." I pause, sorting through my tangled thoughts. "I think I want a home that feels like me for once in my life. Something manageable that I can afford without help. But what if she's right? What if I'm being selfish and Alana would be better off in the big house with all the extras?"

Karen tilts her head, considering. "You know, when Susan and I first got together, her kids were teenagers. Everyone had opinions about what they needed—her ex, her parents, even the kids themselves."

"What did you do?" I ask, leaning forward.

"Susan listened to everyone, then did what felt right to her. She knew her kids better than anyone." Karen reaches over and squeezes my hand. "The thing about parenting is that nobody knows your child like you do. Not even grandparents, no matter how well-intentioned."

"But what if I'm wrong?"

"Then you'll figure it out and adjust. That's what parents do." She smiles. "And don't you think she needs a mother who's happy and confident in her own life more than she needs a pool?"

The weight on my chest lightens slightly. "So you think I should trust my gut?"

"I think your gut has been ignored long enough," Karen says firmly. "You're rediscovering who you are, Deborah. That's a gift to your daughter, not a punishment."

I let out a long breath. "I needed to hear that."

"Besides," Karen adds with a wink, "teenagers don't care about square footage. They care about privacy and Wi-Fi."

We both laugh, and I feel the tension in my shoulders release. "My mother's going to be insufferable about this."

"Probably," Karen agrees cheerfully. "But you'll survive. And hey, speaking of survival..." She leans forward conspiratorially. "What are you doing Thursday night?"

"Probably watching reality TV upstairs. Why?"

"Because I've got something to take your mind off all of this."

I narrow my eyes at her. That sounds like a weak excuse to get me to do something she wants. She knows I'm onto her and she grins back at me.

"Okay," I say, "What is it?"

"A blind date."

I can't help laughing. "Karen, you are out of your mind."

"Guilty. But hear me out. You need to meet people around town. He's reliable, friendly, easy to get along with, and he knows everyone. I could see you two having a great time together. It'll be low pressure, just get out and have a little fun."

I have to admit that does sound nice. I don't know anyone anymore and I need to get grounded in the community.

"Okay fine," I say.

"Thursday night, I'll send you details."

As Karen returns to her desk, humming to herself, I realize I feel lighter than I have in days. The house dilemma suddenly seems manageable. My mother will always have opinions—that's just who she is—but I don't have to let them become my reality.

For the first time in a long time, I'm making choices based on what I want, not what others expect of me. It's terrifying and exhilarating all at once.

"Oh," Karen says, not looking up from her brochures. "His name is Daniel."

I smile, as I always do when I hear that name. It makes me think of my own Danny from so many years ago.

Suddenly, I'm seventeen again, sitting on the hood of Danny's beat-up Chevy Nova, the metal still warm from the afternoon sun. We're parked at the edge of the beach, watching the sun sink into the harbor, painting the water gold and crimson.

"You really think Harvard's gonna take you?" Danny asks, his fingers laced through mine, our shoulders touching. His voice isn't doubtful—just curious, like he's trying to picture me there.

"Early decision," I say, trying to sound more confident than I feel. "My dad says with my grades and extracurriculars, I've got a shot." I don't mention how my father talks about Harvard like it's our family birthright, not a choice.

Danny nods, his thumb tracing circles on my palm. "You'll get in. You're the smartest person I know."

I turn to look at him, this boy with perpetually grease-stained fingernails and a smile that makes my stomach flip. He's wearing his favorite Metallica t-shirt, the one with the frayed collar. His dark hair falls across his forehead, and I resist the urge to push it back.

"What about you?" I ask. "Still thinking trade school?"

He shrugs, eyes on the horizon. "Dad says there's always work for a guy who can fix things. College isn't for everyone. Besides, somebody's gotta stay here and keep everything running. The city isn't far, we'll still be together all the time."

I try to picture it—him visiting me in Boston, me coming home on the weekends— but it's all cloudy in my mind. And I can't help thinking of my father's lecture about Joel Klein who is going pre-med. My parents have always said I should marry Jewish and bring more Jewish babies into the world.

As the last sliver of sun disappears, Danny pulls me closer. "Race you to the water?" he challenges, his eyes bright with mischief.

"You're on," I laugh, already sliding off the hood.

We run down the grassy hill toward the narrow strip of beach, laughing and stumbling. Danny lets me win—I know he does—but when he catches up, lifting me off my feet in a spinning hug, I don't care.

Standing ankle-deep in the cold Atlantic, his arms around my waist, I feel both anchored and adrift. This moment is perfect, but the future looms like storm clouds on the horizon.

It was devastatingly hard to break up with him but that puppy love of teenagers isn't built to last and I know that I freed him up to find someone better suited to his life. I like to imagine him sometimes, living in the town where we grew up, married to a gregarious woman with big hair, four or five kids under foot. During lonely nights after Joel had fallen asleep, the only thing that brought me solace was imagining the chaotic and joyful life I was sure Danny had found.

Finally I pull myself up out of the armchair and head back to my room to look at more listings for houses and job applications.

Danny

Karen picked a nice place a couple of towns over. If it were left up to me I would have just met up with my date at The Steamy Beans cafe but this is probably better. I leave early to get there first. I don't know if Karen told her friend about the wheelchair and it doesn't really matter since it's a favor, not a real date. Still, I always feel like I have a strategic advantage if I don't have my dinner companion watching me wheel across the restaurant, maneuvering between tables and chairs.

I ask the hostess to remove the chair on the far side of the table and I slide into its place. While I wait, I arrange and rearrange the place setting and ask the waitress to bring waters. At the table next to me a couple around my age is feeding each other bites of their dinners and giggling. I wonder if I would have still had that energy with Deb if we stayed together all these years.

Because I'm thinking about her, at first I think I'm mishearing when it sounds like her voice at the hostess stand but then I look over. The woman at the hostess stand turns, and my heart stops for a second. That profile—the slight tilt of her head, the way she tucks her hair behind one ear.

It's actually her. Deborah is my Deb. Thirty-some years later and I recognize her instantly. Her chestnut hair, once wild and untamed, now falls in smooth waves to her shoulders. The girl in faded jeans and ruffled blouses has transformed into a woman in a tailored navy dress that hugs her still-slender frame. Different, yet unmistakable—those same hazel eyes that used to crinkle at the corners when she laughed.

Panic seizes my chest like a vise grip. Her first look at me can't be in a wheelchair. I push my feet onto the floor, my leg muscles trembling with the effort, and place my sweating palms flat on the white tablecloth. I lever my body upright, knuckles blanching as I grip the edge.

She's crossing the polished hardwood floor as the hostess points in my direction. Our eyes lock and she freezes mid-stride, like a deer caught in headlights. Her lips part just a bit, the lipstick a subtle rose shade I would never have seen on the girl I knew.

"Danny?" she whispers, her voice carrying across the murmur of the restaurant. One manicured hand flies to her chest, fingers splayed against her collarbone. She advances, arm already extending for an embrace.

But if I release my death grip on the table I'll collapse, so I remain rigid, watching her gesture hang suspended between us. A small crease forms between her brows as confusion flickers across her face. Then her gaze drops, taking in the wheelchair half-hidden behind me. Her outstretched arm falls slowly, like a deflating balloon, and she slides into the seat across from me. Shakily, I lower myself back down, the chair creaking beneath me.

"I can't believe it's you," Deb says.

I know what she means. I can't help thinking I may have had a stroke and be hallucinating all of this. "I didn't know you knew Karen," I say finally.

Deborah nods. "She was my RA freshman year of college. How do you know Karen?"

A nice safe topic. "I do all the maintenance work at The Whispering Pines."

"Oh. So did you hurt your foot on the job?"

"No. The chair is permanent but I don't want to talk about that."

"Oh. Okay."

Just in time, the waitress comes by to take our dinner orders and pour some wine. I'm tempted to bail but I can't just leave with no information like whether I'm going to start seeing her around town.

"So life with Joel wasn't all it was cracked up to be?" I'm instantly sorry I made her look uncomfortable.

"You don't want to hear about that," she says down at her napkin.

"Maybe just the break-up bit." I swirl my glass and grin at her.

She laughs a little bit then but it's strained.

Our food arrives, giving me a moment to collect my thoughts. This is surreal—sitting across from Deborah Cohen after thirty years, both of us so different yet somehow the same. I watch as she takes a bite of her salmon, the same little furrow appearing between her eyebrows that I remember from when she'd concentrate on homework.

Deb twirls her wine glass between manicured fingers, the burgundy liquid catching the restaurant's soft lighting. "You know," she says, her lips curving into a gentle smile, "I always thought you'd be married to a local girl with a big personality who runs your life with military precision and you love it."

I lean back in my wheelchair. "Gave it a lot of thought, have you?"

"Yeah," she says quietly, her gaze dropping to the tablecloth where she traces invisible patterns with her fingertip. "I have."

The candle between us flickers, casting shadows across her face. "I thought you'd be traveling the world with Joel, showing your kids world culture up close," I say.

"We did do some of that."

"With kids?" I ask.

She nods, a genuine smile warming her features. "With one kid. I have a daughter. Alana. She's fifteen." Her eyes flick up to mine. "You?"

"No." I shake my head. "Never married, no kids. Just me keeping things running around town."

The silence settles between us like dust. Her eyes dart to my wheelchair and then away, her fingers fidgeting with her napkin. I know she's dying to ask about it again but she respects that I said I didn't want to talk about it and swallows the question down with a sip of wine.

I tap my knuckles lightly against the table. "Your parents thought I was the bad influence. Maybe they had it backwards all along. Maybe you were the bad influence on me."

Deb's eyebrows shoot up. "Me? I was the student council president!"

"Exactly. The perfect cover. Who suggested we sneak onto the football field that night after homecoming? Not me."

A blush creeps across her cheeks. "That was one time."

"And whose idea was it to skip calculus to drive to the beach in April? When it was fifty degrees?"

"We had jackets," she protests, but she's laughing now, the tension between us finally easing.

"And let's not forget who convinced me to climb onto the roof of the library to watch the meteor shower." I shake my head in mock disapproval. "You nearly got us both killed."

"The view was worth it," she says softly, and something in her tone makes my chest tighten.

Our eyes meet across the table, and for a moment, we're those kids again—before life pulled us in different directions, before everything changed.

The waitress appears with dessert menus, breaking the spell.

We order coffee instead of dessert, and conversation flows more easily now. She tells me about her accounting practice, about moving back to start fresh. I tell her about my handyman business, how I've built it over the years.

After dinner I pick up the check and wave away her protest. "Please, I insist." I gesture toward the exit. "After you." My eyes flick to her back as she turns, my shoulders relaxing once she's facing away. I don't think I'd be able to move if I knew she was behind watching me. My palms slide along the push rims of my chair as I follow her out.

Outside, goosebumps rise on my forearms as a breeze carries the scent of salt water from the harbor. The parking lot stretches before us, my wheels crunching over scattered gravel between islands of lamplight. I match her pace, keeping slightly behind her left shoulder.

She stops at a red sedan and pauses, her fingers worrying at her keys. Finally she says, "It was really great to see you, Danny. I'm glad we could catch up."

"Me too," I say.

I return home alone and I can hear my own blood pounding in my ears. Emotions and thoughts are fighting to be heard in my brain and I don't know how to identify any of them.

This time when I sink into my recliner, I don't turn on the TV. I open the little drawer in the end table next to the recliner and pull out a strip of photos—three black-and-white squares, edges curled from years of being stuffed in wallets or boxes or, for a while, taped to the inside of my locker. The top one is the best: me and Deb with our cheeks smushed together, both of us grinning so wide our eyes are almost shut. In the next, she's sticking out her tongue and I'm feigning horror, which makes me laugh now because I remember how she'd insisted on being "the silly one" in every photo. The last square is blurry because just before the camera flashed, she reached over and kissed my cheek, and I jerked like I'd been shocked.

I study them like a crime scene, trying to reconstruct the evidence of who we were. I can't believe how young we are in the pictures—thin and baby-faced, the kind of young that seems impossible once you've crossed a certain threshold into adulthood. My hair is longer than I remember ever having it, my nose unbroken from a fight that wouldn't happen for another year. She's wearing a ridiculous plastic tiara from the fair, the kind you win by throwing darts at balloons. I remember how she'd made me put it on after the photos, and how I wore it for the rest of the night just because it made her laugh so hard she got the hiccups.

I try to recall what it felt like to be that open, that unguarded. I remember the giddy joy of the Fourth of July fair—how the air smelled like popcorn and fried dough, how the whole town sparkled under a sky that seemed big enough to swallow every worry we had. Everything was so easy with her back then, no second-guessing, no waiting for the other shoe to drop. Even holding hands was thrilling, like we were the first people who ever thought of it.

I look at myself in the reflection of the living room window, at the way my shoulders hunch now and how the corners of my mouth seem to pull downward even when I'm not thinking about anything sad. I wonder how the boy in these pictures would feel if he saw me now—if he knew the punctured timeline that lay ahead. A marriage that never happened, a job that turned into something else, a body that refused to cooperate. Would he recognize me at all? Would he even want to?

The weirdest part is that I never really expected to see Deb again. I'd written her off as a closed chapter, a sweet kid who moved away and settled into a more glittery, ambitious version of herself. It never occurred to me that our paths would cross again, or that it would feel so... unfinished.

I run my thumb across the photo strip, remembering the way she used to laugh—wholehearted, like the concept of embarrassment was foreign to her. The way she'd look at me and make me feel like I was the only person in a crowded room, even at a noisy bonfire party or in her parents' packed kitchen.

I rest my head against the back of the recliner, the photo strip balanced on my stomach. I think about the way Deb looked at me across the table tonight, her eyes full of questions she didn't ask, and I wonder if she was remembering the same things I am. I wonder if the girl in these photos is still somewhere inside her, or if the world sanded those edges down like it did with me. Maybe that's why seeing her hit so hard. It's not just nostalgia— it's the realization that some part of me still believes in the person I was when I was with her.

For a long time, I just sit there, letting the silence fill up around me and I can't shake the question: if you could go back and warn yourself, would you? Or would you let yourself believe, just for a few more months, that the world was going to give you everything you hoped for?

I press the photo strip back into the drawer, telling myself that tonight was just a fluke, a random collision of old lives in a new place. But I know better. The ache in my chest isn't going anywhere.

As terrible as it is for my bladder and my body, I end up falling asleep in the recliner.

Deborah

The morning light filters through lace curtains, casting delicate patterns across the bedspread. I lie still for a moment, watching dust motes dance in the sunbeams, before the memories of last night flood back. Danny. After all these years—Danny Wallace sitting across from me at dinner, those same kind eyes in a face that's weathered life's storms.

I slide out of bed, careful not to wake Alana, who's sprawled across her side with one arm flung dramatically over her face. It's true what they say, teenagers need extra sleep. The wooden floor is cool beneath my bare feet as I pad to the bathroom to splash water on my face.

When I make my way downstairs, the scent of coffee draws me to the kitchen where Karen stands at the counter, her back to me as she arranges fresh-baked muffins on a plate.

"Morning," I say, my voice still husky with sleep.

Karen whirls around, eyes bright with curiosity. "Well, good morning! I was wondering when you'd surface." She slides a steaming mug toward me. "Coffee?"

"God, yes." I wrap my hands around the warmth, inhaling deeply.

"So..." Karen draws out the word, eyebrows raised expectantly. "How was dinner?"

I sink onto one of the kitchen chairs and wait while an elderly couple staying at the B&B comes in to pick out muffins and refresh their coffees. As they leave, Susan comes in carrying a tray of used teacups.

"Well, dinner was interesting," I say. I think Karen is going to implode if I don't hurry up and get to the point. "Danny and I know each other. He was my high school sweetheart."

Karen's mouth drops open. The muffin she's holding freezes midway to the plate. "What?!"

"That must have been quite a shock," Susan says. She puts down her tray and sits beside me, a hand on my shoulder.

"Things didn't end on the best note," I admit. "But we were teenagers. I mean, who gets that right?"

"And now you're both back here." Susan says quietly. "Seems like a sign of something."

"It's complicated," I say, thinking of the wheelchair I hadn't expected, the way his strong hands gripped the table as he struggled to stand.

"Was it weird? Seeing him again?" Karen asks, joining us at the table.

"Yes. No. Both, I guess." I let my gaze drift to the window, where a pair of crows squabble in the brittle winter sunshine. "He's different, but still so much the same. Can I ask you something?"

Karen nods, picking a crumb from her sleeve. "Sure. Shoot. But if it's a quiz about his favorite pizza topping, I already lost."

"Do you know what happened to him?"

"You mean the wheelchair?" Karen leans back, then forward, then drums her fingers on the tabletop, her brow knitting. "Actually...I have no idea," she says at last. "He never talks about himself. Not about that, anyway. He'll tell you how to fix a leaky pipe in the dead of January or which hardware store has the best snow shovels, but anything personal?" She shakes her head. "Nope. Guy's a vault. He's been disabled since I got here at least. How long ago was that?"

"Twenty-five years," Susan supplies.

"Oh fuck," Karen mutters.

I chew on that, trying to think if I heard anything about him in the last twenty-five years. But I know I haven't. Everyone else wanted to keep me away from him and I never looked him up because I wanted to believe in the future I imagined for him. If I searched for him or asked about him, that illusion would have been shattered and I wouldn't be able to keep believing that I did the right thing breaking up with him.

"So I take it that's new since you last saw him?" Karen says.

I nod. "I had no idea."

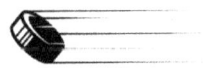

The moment I set eyes on the house, I know it's the one.

It's tucked away on a quiet street lined with old maples, their branches stretching like protective arms over the sidewalk. Allison is still talking about square footage and property taxes, but I've stopped listening.

"It needs work," Allison warns, noting my expression as we walk up the cracked flagstone path. "A lot of work, actually."

But I barely hear her. The little Cape Cod cottage stands before me like something from a storybook, with its weathered gray shingles and pink shutters hanging slightly crooked against white-painted clapboard. There are even matching pink windowboxes with remnants of pink drifting roses. The front garden is overgrown with wildflowers and herbs gone feral, but I can already picture Alana and me taming it next spring, bringing order while keeping its wild charm.

"The previous owner was elderly," Allison explains, fumbling with the lockbox. "She lived here for nearly sixty years before passing last winter. Her children decided to sell rather than renovate."

The door creaks open, and I step inside, inhaling the distinctive scent of old wood and dust. Sunlight streams through wavy glass windowpanes, casting golden pools on the wide-plank pine floors. They're scratched and worn but solid beneath my feet.

"The kitchen needs a complete overhaul," Allison says apologetically, leading me through a small living room with a massive stone fireplace.

She's right. The kitchen is a time capsule from 1975: avocado green appliances, laminate countertops with metal edging, linoleum peeling up at the corners. But the windows face east, and morning light floods the space. I can already see myself here with coffee, watching the sunrise.

"The roof was replaced ten years ago, but there is a patch where the shingles need replacing, the electrical needs updating, and the plumbing..." She trails off with a grimace.

I run my hand along a built-in cabinet, feeling the smooth wood beneath my fingertips. "How many bedrooms?"

"Two upstairs, though they're small and one downstairs. There's a half bath up there too, and a full bath down here that definitely needs work."

We climb the narrow staircase, each step sighing under our weight. The upstairs is all sloped ceilings and dormer windows, creating cozy nooks that make the small rooms feel intentional rather than cramped. The larger bedroom has a window seat overlooking the backyard with its ancient oak tree.

"Alana would love this," I murmur, mostly to myself.

"The asking price reflects the condition," Allison says carefully. "But even with renovations, you'd still be well under what you'd pay for something move-in ready in this neighborhood."

Back downstairs, I wander from room to room, mentally cataloging what needs to be done. New wiring. Updated plumbing. Kitchen renovation. Bathroom overhaul. Fresh paint everywhere. It's overwhelming, but also exhilarating.

This house has good bones and a soul. I can feel it in the way the afternoon light slants through the windows, in the solid thunk of the doors as they close, in the worn spots on the stair treads where countless feet have traveled up and down.

"I'd like to make an offer," I say, surprising myself with my certainty.

Allison blinks. "Don't you want to think about it? Or at least bring your daughter to see it?"

I shake my head, smiling. "I know it's right. This is home."

Later, when I tell my parents about my decision, they're predictably horrified.

"You put an offer on a house without consulting us?" My father's voice crackles with indignation over the speakerphone. "Without even having it inspected?"

"The inspection is scheduled for next week," I explain, trying to keep my voice level. "And I didn't need to consult you because I'm buying it with my own money."

"But Debbie," my mother chimes in, "you said yourself it needs everything! The cost of renovations alone—"

"Will be spread out over time," I finish for her. "I don't need it perfect right away. Just livable."

"This is that midlife crisis talking," my father mutters. "First the divorce, now this money pit—"

"It's not a money pit, Dad. It's a home. My home." I take a deep breath. "And it's not a crisis. It's me finally figuring out what I want."

The silence that follows speaks volumes. What I want has never mattered to them. Probably because what they wanted never mattered to anyone in their lives either.

"Will you at least bring Alana by to see it before the inspection?" my mother finally asks, her tone making it clear she expects my daughter to talk sense into me.

"Of course," I say.

When I hang up, I feel lighter than I have in months. The cottage needs work—just like me. We'll heal together, this old house and I, finding our way back to solid ground one repair at a time.

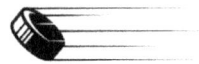

The next day, Alana is quieter than usual when I pick her up from an afternoon with my parents. She's wearing a new outfit I've never seen before—a frilly blouse and pleated skirt that looks nothing like her usual style. My mother hovers in the doorway, beaming.

"Doesn't she look beautiful?" Mom asks. "We had such fun shopping today."

I bite my tongue. The outfit is perfectly nice, just not Alana. But I won't make a scene, not when I'm about to show her our potential new home.

"You look lovely," I tell my daughter, who shrugs uncomfortably.

In the car, she tugs at the collar of the blouse. "Bubbe said this is what girls my age wear."

"You can wear whatever makes you comfortable," I reply carefully.

She nods, looking out the window. "So where is this house you bought without telling me?"

I wince at her phrasing—so like my parents'. "I haven't bought it yet. I made an offer, and I wanted you to see it before we move forward."

When we pull up to the cottage, Alana's expression is unreadable. We walk up the path together, and I unlock the door with the key Allison left for us.

"It's... small," she says as we step inside.

"Cozy," I correct, trying not to sound defensive. "And it's just the two of us." I try not to think about how soon it will be just me. My little girl is growing up fast and she'll be out on her own making her own life and her own mistakes before I know it.

I watch her face as she moves through the rooms, trailing her fingers along the walls like I did. When she reaches the upstairs bedroom with the window seat, she pauses, looking out at the oak tree.

"This would be your room," I tell her. "If you want it."

She sits on the window seat, testing it. "It's kind of cool," she admits reluctantly. "But Bubbe says the schools here aren't as good."

I sit beside her, our shoulders touching. "The schools are fine. Different, but good. And this place—" I gesture around us. "This place could be ours. Really ours."

"It needs a lot of work," she points out.

"I know. We'll do it together. Learn as we go."

She's quiet for a long moment, then turns to me with a small smile that reminds me so much of her younger self. "Can I paint my room whatever color I want?"

I laugh, relief washing through me. "Absolutely. Even if it's black."

"I was thinking purple, actually." She leans against me, and I wrap my arm around her shoulders.

"Purple it is."

Danny

I'm teaching a shop class at the high school and when I see the new girl in the class I know who she is immediately. She looks like Joel. But I won't let it distract me as I catch her up to speed. Whatever history I have with her parents doesn't need to come into this space.

"Morning, folks," I call out, and the chatter dies down. "We're continuing with our cutting board projects today. New faces, see me before you start."

She approaches my desk hesitantly after the others scatter to their workstations.

"I'm Alana Klein," she says, voice steady despite the nerves I can see in her fidgeting hands. "I just transferred."

"Mr. Wallace," I reply, not letting on that I know exactly who she is. "Welcome to Woodshop. The class is halfway through a cutting board project, but we can get you caught up."

I lead her to an empty workstation, conscious of the curious glances from the other students. Small towns, everyone's interested in the new kid.

"Ever worked with wood before?" I ask.

She shakes her head. "No. My dad's not really the handy type." A slight grimace follows, like she's said more than she intended.

"That's alright. We'll start with safety." I demonstrate how to use the push sticks, keeping my voice even, professional. "Always keep your hands at least six inches from the blade."

I guide her through measuring and marking her board, showing her how to use the square to make precise lines. Her hands are tentative at first, but she's a quick learner.

"You've got a good eye," I tell her when she lines everything up perfectly on her first try.

She looks surprised by the compliment. "Thanks. I did take art classes at my old school."

"That'll serve you well here. Woodworking's as much art as science."

As the class progresses, I circle the room, helping where needed, but I find myself drawn back to Alana's station. Not because she needs more help—she doesn't—but because I can't stop seeing echoes of Deb in her movements. The way she bites her lower lip when concentrating. The little sigh of satisfaction when a cut comes out clean.

When it's time for her first pass on the bandsaw, I sit close by. "Nice and slow," I instruct. "Let the blade do the work."

Her cut wavers slightly. "Sorry," she mutters.

"Nothing to be sorry for. First cuts are always the hardest." I demonstrate on a scrap piece. "Try again."

Her second attempt is better. By the third, she's got it.

"You're a natural," I tell her, and mean it.

"My mom said this class would be good for me," she says, carefully sanding the edge she's just cut. "She said it teaches patience."

I swallow hard. "Your mom sounds wise."

"She has her moments," Alana says with that particular tone teenagers reserve for parents they love but would never admit to respecting. "We just moved back here. She grew up near Cedar Harbor."

"Is that right?" I keep my voice casual. "How's she finding it, being back?"

Alana shrugs. "Weird, I think. She keeps having these moments where she stares at random buildings like they're going to talk to her."

I can't help but smile at that. "Lots of memories in old buildings."

The bell rings, saving me from saying more. The students begin cleaning their stations, putting tools away.

"You're doing great," I tell Alana as she carefully brushes sawdust into the trash. "By next class, you'll be caught up with everyone else."

"Thanks, Mr. Wallace." She hesitates, then adds, "This was actually kind of fun."

"Glad to hear it." I watch her join the stream of students heading for the door, her ponytail swinging.

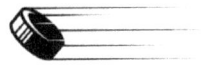

I pick up my phone to an unknown number. "Dan's handy, what can I do for you?"

"Turns out you're the highest rated handyman in a twenty mile radius...by a lot."

I smile. Deb. "Glad to hear it," I say.

"I'm going to put an offer on a place, want to come tell me if that's a terrible idea?"

"I can tell you that from here. What do you mean you found a place already? I don't remember you being impulsive."

There's a slight pause and then her voice softens. "Maybe I've learned that the first really can be the best."

I'm not touching that with a ten foot pole. "Text me the address," I say and hang up.

I recognize the town name. It's less than twenty minutes from here if Rt 2 is behaving itself.

For a while, I sit in my empty classroom, surrounded by the smell of fresh-cut wood and the fine dust that hangs in the air, catching sunlight through the windows. I think about coincidences and second chances, about the strange circles life draws when you're not looking.

Deborah

I get back to my new place and see there's a ladder leaning against the side of the cottage. When I get out of my car I notice that it's bungee corded to the picket fence and a wheelchair has been abandoned at the bottom. Danny's truck is parked around the side of the house in the tall grass. I walk over to the bottom of the ladder and look up, lifting a hand to shade my eyes from the sun.

He's up there all right, nailing shingles onto the roof. Even from here I can tell there's something a little off about his legs and the way he's sitting. I'm so curious about what happened to them but he said he didn't want to talk about so I won't ask again.

When he notices me watching he puts down the shingle, puts his hammer into a loop in the cross-chest tool belt he's wearing, and shimmies his way to the edge of the roof. My breath stops as I watch him grab the top rung of the ladder and let his body fall off the side, dangling in the air from only the strength of his arms.

The ladder sways dramatically but is stopped from tipping over by the bungee cords on each side as he moves down it like vertical monkey bars, his massive arms moving with perfect confidence. My jaw is hanging open and I don't even notice until I try to speak.

"You always did have more bravery than sense," I finally manage.

He swings back into his wheelchair on solid ground and spins to face me. "Like you're not exactly the same way."

I try and fail to avoid smiling. "How's the roof?"

"Not as bad as I feared. I'll finish that spot and then do one more patch and you'll be all set for the winter. When is the closing?"

"Ten days," I say.

He wipes his brow with the back of one hairy arm. "That's fast."

"Just what I need. It's felt for way too long like my life is in a holding pattern."

We both look at the cottage. "It's very you," Danny says.

It is. And for the first time my home can be exactly what I want it to be, no compromises.

"You know what I miss?" I say.

"What?"

"Racing you in the pool."

Danny laughs. "Hey, I was just swimming laps. I couldn't help that you're insanely competitive."

"Liar."

His phone buzzes in his front shirt pocket and I see over his shoulder someone named Kevin Murphy is calling. Danny answers on speaker phone and there's something about that level of trust that warms my heart.

"What's up, Murph?"

"Team has a huge opportunity. We can play our first real game if we can come up with a sixth player in time."

"When is it?"

"Two weeks."

Danny sighs and runs his fingers roughly through his hair, leaving it in tousled disarray. "That's nuts."

"I know. But if anyone can find a player, it's you. You know people."

Suddenly the memory of swimming laps next to Danny gives me an idea. I touch his shoulder and lean over to speak quietly into his ear. "Could I play?"

"What was that?" Murph's voice warbles through the phone.

Danny raises an eyebrow at me and I eagerly nod towards the phone, encouraging him to suggest it to his friend. "My friend Deb wants to play."

"Okay, will that work?"

"Well, she's never played before and she's not disabled, so you tell me."

There's a pause for a long moment and Danny and I both look at the phone waiting for the verdict.

Finally Murph says, "It's not like we're a pro team. I don't think it's a big deal to cheat a little. Can she make it to practice tonight?"

"Yes!" I say, "I'll be there."

"You don't even know what time it is," Danny says.

"'I'll make it work.'" I can't tell if he's upset at the idea of me playing with him. It may have been going too far to push my way into his hobby like that and even though we seem to have fallen into an easy rapport, that doesn't mean he wants to see me all the time. I really need to make more friends around here so Karen and Danny don't feel like they have to take care of me and meet all my social needs.

Danny hangs up the phone and before he can say anything I say, "I'm sorry. I shouldn't have invited myself along. That was presumptuous."

Danny laughs. "You haven't changed a bit, Debbie."

"Neither have you." I gesture toward the ladder. "Still taking unnecessary risks to show off."

"Who says they're unnecessary? That roof won't fix itself." His eyes crinkle at the corners when he smiles, lines I don't remember from before.

"Fine, but next time maybe use a harness or something? For my blood pressure's sake?"

"Worried about me?" he teases.

"Someone has to be." The words come out more serious than I intended.

A moment passes between us, weighted with thirty years of unspoken history. I clear my throat. "So, what time is practice? And what do I need to bring?"

"Seven at the rec center. Just wear something comfortable. They've got sleds and gear you can borrow." He checks his watch. "I should get back up there and finish this section before it gets too late."

"Need a spotter?" I ask, only half-joking.

"Nah, I've got a system." He gestures to the bungee cords. "Been doing this for decades."

I watch as he hauls himself back onto the ladder with impressive upper body strength, ascending rung by rung until he's back on the roof. There's something hypnotic about the fluid way he moves.

"See you tonight!" I call up before heading inside.

The cottage is still mostly empty boxes, but it already feels more like home than my pristine suburban house ever did. I run my hand along the kitchen counter, mind racing with excitement about tonight. It's been years since I tried a new sport, even longer since I had something that was just for me—not for Alana, not for work, not for my parents' approval.

I wonder what Alana will say when I tell her I'm joining a sled hockey team. She'll probably think I'm having some kind of midlife crisis. Maybe I am. But as I look around at this beautiful mess of a cottage, at the new life I'm building piece by piece, I can't help but think that some crises are worth having.

Danny

Before practice, Murph waves his stick in the air. "Huddle up!" The blades of our sleds carve semicircles in the ice as we gather around him. His breath forms small clouds in the cold rink air.

"Got news," he says, tapping his gloved hand against his thigh. "Bedford called. They've got an opening on the 25th if we can field six players." He nods toward me. "Danny's bringing someone to fill our last spot."

A few grunts and nods ripple through our circle. Mark adjusts his helmet strap. Jack's eyebrows raise slightly.

"She's coming tonight," Murph continues, "She is able-bodied, so we wanted to check with all of you how

you feel about that. Obviously it's against the rules to
have an abled player on a sled hockey team."

"Would probably take up all the points," Robbie
says. "You get an able-bodied player, but they're the
only player."

I picture Deb alone on the ice, frantically paddling
her sled against six opponents, and a laugh escapes me.

Murph shrugs. "It's not the Paralympics. Just a
friendly game." His eyes scan our faces. "Anyone have
a problem with it?"

Heads shake. Shoulders shrug.

Murph claps his hands together. "Great." He gestures toward the equipment room, and I follow him to
drag out the spare sled.

Deb arrives shortly and she's all smiles and charm. I
introduce her as an old friend and everyone takes to her
immediately. I don't know why but it makes me feel a
swell of pride in my chest. Like I'm proud that I have
good taste in friends, I guess.

While everyone else starts warm-ups, I show Deborah
the basics of the sled and the sticks and how it all works.

"So I sit here?"

"Yep. And I'm going to strap your legs down."

"So I'm not tempted to use them?"

"Nah, we all have our legs strapped down. Well, all of us that have legs. Don't want them flopping around or flying out of sled on impact."

"Impact? Is this as violent as regular hockey?"

"It can be but we're a no contact team. Still, impacts can happen by accident. Not just from other players but from the walls, equipment, tipping over."

Her face is going pale.

"Let's just get out there and start," I say.

"Am I going to let everyone down?" she asks quietly. She's looking past me to where the guys are running drills.

"The alternative to you is having no one, so whatever you can do is going to be great."

I may have spoken too soon. The moment I let go of the sled, she immediately tips to the side and her shoulder crashes into the ice.

"You okay?" I ask.

"Ouch," she says, but she lets me show her how to push back up with her arms and try again to balance on the single blade beneath the sled. Her legs keep trying to help, straining against the straps intuitively.

A few moments later, Murph glides over to check on us. He's the one who taught the rest of us so I've never tried to show someone how to do this. "Hey," Murph says, his tone more patient than I expected. "It's her first time. Remember how we all looked our first day?"

I nod, grateful for his understanding. "She just needs to get the feel of it."

"You're thinking too much," Murph tells Deborah, positioning his sled next to hers. "Your body wants to balance naturally. Just let it happen."

Deb's face is flushed, a mix of embarrassment and determination I recognize from high school. She was never one to back down from a challenge.

"Like this?" she asks, shifting her weight and managing to stay upright for a solid ten seconds before wobbling again.

"Better," Murph says. "Now try moving. Small pushes with the picks on your sticks."

I watch her struggle to coordinate the movements, pushing with one stick while holding the other end for balance, then switching. Each attempt sends her lurching in unpredictable directions. Twice more she tips over completely, landing hard on the ice.

"You sure about this?" I ask quietly when I help her up the third time.

Her jaw sets in that stubborn way I remember so well. "Absolutely."

After twenty minutes of basic movement, Murph signals it's time to join the others for passing drills. I catch his eye and shake my head slightly.

"She's not ready," I murmur when he skates closer.

"Nobody ever is," he answers with a shrug. "Sometimes you learn by doing."

I know he's right, but something protective flares in my chest as I watch Deb wobble her way toward the group. She's trying so hard, her face a mask of concentration as she navigates across the ice.

The guys form a circle, and I position myself opposite Deb, figuring I can at least make sure my passes to her are manageable. But when Mark's gentle pass slides her way, she swings wildly, missing the puck entirely and nearly toppling over.

"Sorry!" she calls, her voice echoing in the cavernous rink.

"No worries," Jack says, retrieving the puck. "Took me weeks to hit anything."

The next pass comes from Robbie, harder than it should be. I shoot him a warning look as the puck zips past Deb before she can react.

"Slow it down," I call out, more edge to my voice than intended.

Practice continues this way, Deb struggling with even the most basic elements while the rest of us modify our play to accommodate her. She's a natural athlete, I remember that much from high school, but this is different. This requires a complete rewiring of instincts.

By the time Murph calls for a water break, Deb's hair is plastered to her forehead with sweat, and her breathing comes in sharp bursts. I wheel over to the bench where she's parked her sled.

"How you holding up?" I ask, passing her a water bottle.

She takes a long drink before answering. "I'm going to get back out and practice some more." She pushes off alone on the ice.

Watching someone who is brand new at sled hockey is entertaining in and off itself. Deb is careening around the rink, picking up speed much faster than she can manage, and frequently tipping over or crashing into the walls with an adorable shriek.

"She might be even worse than Jack was," Murph comments as we all sit and watch.

"I resent that," Jack says, but he's got an amused smile on his face and there's no venom in his voice.

"We're not going to get to play a game, are we?" Mark says.

"I'll work with her," I say. "I'll get her up to speed."

"All I can say is...good luck," Robbie laughs. He pushes his sticks against the ice and glides out towards her. I watch as he tries to steer her around like he's some kind of sheepdog on ice and they both laugh.

This is going to be quite a challenge but with the opportunity to finally play a real hockey game on the line, I'm up for it.

Deborah

My mother's front door is heavier than I remember, solid mahogany with beveled glass inserts that cost more than my first month's rent in Boston. I press the doorbell and hear the same musical chime echoing through the foyer that I've heard since childhood. Some things never change, especially in my parents' world where consistency is valued above all else. I shift my weight from one foot to the other, suddenly feeling like I'm sixteen again, about to confess to breaking curfew. Except I'm fifty-three, and what I've broken is my marriage.

The door swings open, and there stands my mother, perfectly coiffed in a cashmere sweater set and pearls at eleven in the morning. Her eyebrows lift slightly—the Klein family equivalent of a full-body tackle.

"Deborah. You're early." She checks her watch, a delicate gold thing that probably cost as much as my down payment.

"Hi, Mom." I lean in to kiss her cheek. She smells like Chanel No. 5 and disapproval. "I thought we said eleven."

"Eleven-thirty," she corrects, but steps aside to let me in. "Your father's on a call. He'll be down soon."

I follow her through the marble-floored entryway into the living room where everything is cream, beige, or ivory; a testament to my mother's conviction that color is for other people's homes. The furniture is different from my childhood home but somehow exactly the same: expensive, uncomfortable, and arranged for appearances rather than conversation. My parents upgraded to this house five years ago when my father semi-retired from his law practice, but it feels like they've lived here forever.

"Tea?" Mom asks, already pouring from a silver pot into bone china cups that look too fragile to hold liquid.

"Thanks." I sink onto the sofa, trying not to wrinkle anything.

Mom hands me a cup and saucer, watching as I take a sip. "You look tired," she announces, settling into her armchair. "Are you sleeping?"

And so it begins. "I'm fine, Mom. Just busy with the move and getting Alana settled."

"That little cottage." She says it like I've chosen to live in a cardboard box under a bridge. "I still don't understand why you won't consider something in our neighborhood. The Silvermans' daughter just listed her house. Four bedrooms, beautiful yard."

"I don't need four bedrooms. It's just me and Alana, and she's only there on weekdays."

My mother's lips thin to a line so precise it could cut glass. "About that arrangement—"

She's interrupted by my father's entrance. He's wearing khakis and a button-down shirt with a cashmere cardigan—his version of casual—but his posture is all boardroom authority. At seventy-eight, he still stands ramrod straight, still commands every room he enters.

"There she is," he says, coming over to kiss the top of my head. "How's my girl?"

"Hi, Dad." For a moment, I'm genuinely happy to see him. Then he sits down, crosses one leg over the other, and gives me the same evaluating look he gives his opponents in court.

"So," he begins, accepting the cup of tea Mom hands him. "What's the plan, Deborah?"

No small talk, no warm-up. Straight to the inquisition.

"The plan is to get settled in my new house, help Alana adjust to her new school, and find an accounting position nearby."

Dad nods as if I've just presented him with an interesting theory he's about to demolish. "And what about the firm in New York? Surely they'd take you back."

"I worked there through Joel's connections," I remind him. "It wouldn't be comfortable." What I don't say: Joel's colleagues—most of them doctors' wives—would treat me like a pariah, the woman who left the good doctor.

"There are other firms," Dad points out. "With your experience—"

"I'm not commuting from here to New York, that's crazy," I cut in. "I want something local. Something manageable."

"Manageable," Mom repeats, like it's a foreign concept. "Since when do Cohens settle for manageable? You were married to a doctor, Debbie. You had the best."

Since I realized I was suffocating in a life that looked perfect on paper but felt hollow inside. Since I woke up on my fiftieth birthday and couldn't remember the last time I made a decision solely for myself.

"I've been applying to accounting positions around Cedar Harbor," I say instead. "There are a few promising leads."

"Local firms," Dad says flatly. "With what kind of client base?"

"Small businesses, mostly." I take another sip of tea, wishing it were something stronger. "A few larger clients. It's not Manhattan hospitals and medical practices, but it's honest work."

My mother exchanges a look with my father, the kind of silent communication they've perfected over fifty-five years of marriage. I used to envy that connection. Now I wonder if it's just shorthand for mutual judgment.

"We just worry," Mom says, reaching over to pat my knee. "You had such a beautiful life in New York. The brownstone, Joel's attending position at Columbia, the country club membership, that lovely summer house in the Hamptons."

"All Joel's," I remind her. "Not mine."

"But they could have been yours," Dad interjects. "Marriage is about compromise, Debbie. Joel is a respected doctor and he was willing to work through whatever issues you were having."

The familiar pressure builds in my chest, that feeling of being slowly crushed under the weight of their expectations. "Joel was willing to pretend nothing was wrong as long as I played my part."

"And what part was that?" Dad asks, his lawyer voice emerging. "Loving wife? Mother to your child? Partner to a successful physician? What exactly was so unbearable?"

The question hangs in the air, demanding an answer I'm not sure I can articulate. At least not one they would understand. How do I explain that I woke up one morning and realized I'd been sleepwalking through my own life for decades? That the person I'd become was unrecognizable to me?

"I wasn't happy," I finally say. "And neither was Joel, not really. We were just...coexisting."

Mom sighs dramatically. "Happiness comes and goes in a marriage, Deborah. You weather the storms together. Especially when your husband is a doctor—those hours, the stress—it's not easy, but you make it work."

"This wasn't a storm, Mom. It was my life."

"And what about Alana's life?" Dad cuts in. "Have you considered what this is doing to her? Shuttling back and forth on trains, starting a new school, watching her family fall apart? With Joel working those hospital shifts, she needs stability."

The guilt stabs sharp and familiar. "Alana and I have talked a lot about this. She understands more than you think."

"She's fifteen," Mom says dismissively. "She needs stability."

"She has stability. She has me, she has Joel, she has you two, she has the temple community." I set my teacup down with a little more force than intended. "And the arrangement with Joel works. He can't have her during the week anyway—he's barely home before nine most nights, always on call, always at the hospital."

"At least he's working," Dad mutters. "Providing."

"So am I," I snap back, surprising myself with the heat in my voice. "I've always worked."

"Part-time," Mom corrects. "This is different. You'll be her primary caregiver and working full-time. When will you have time to help with her homework? To make proper meals? To be there when she needs you? It's not like when Joel was on call and you could be home."

The same way millions of other single working mothers do it, I want to say. But I know that's not an answer they'll accept. In their world, a mother who chooses career over full-time childrearing is failing at her most fundamental job.

"We're figuring it out together," I say instead. "And she's fifteen, not five. She can microwave her own dinner if I'm running late."

Mom's expression is pained. "Microwave dinners? Alana deserves better than that—she's the daughter of a doctor. You could have stayed in New York, with Joel, and none of this would be necessary."

"Better than what? A mother who's building a life that makes her happy and fulfilled? A mother who's showing her daughter that it's never too late to make a change?"

"A mother who's showing her that commitments don't matter," Dad counters. "That when things get tough, you just walk away, even from someone as good as Joel."

"Is that what you think I did?" I feel heat rising in my cheeks. "You think I just woke up one morning and decided to throw away thirty years of marriage to Dr. Joel Klein on a whim?"

"Then explain it to us," Mom pleads. "Help us understand."

But I can't. Not when they've already decided that my choices are wrong, that the only acceptable path is the one they would choose for me. Not when every conversation circles back to the same conclusion: I've failed, and my only redemption lies in returning to Joel.

"I need to be going," I say, setting my cup on the coffee table and standing up. "I have an appointment."

"You just got here," Mom protests.

"I know, and I'm sorry, but I really do have somewhere to be." The lie comes easily, practiced from years of creating gentle excuses to escape uncomfortable situations.

Dad stands too, hands in his pockets. "You know we only want what's best for you, Debbie."

And there it is: the phrase that suddenly crystallizes everything. What's best for you. It sounds like love, like concern, but for the first time, I hear the subtext clearly: What's best for you according to us. What's best for you as we define it.

"I know you think you do," I say carefully. "But I'm the only one who can decide what's actually best for me."

Mom's lips purse. "When you've calmed down and thought this through—"

"I'm not upset, Mom." I meet her gaze steadily. "I'm just finally seeing things clearly."

She blinks, momentarily thrown by my directness. We don't speak to each other this way in our family. We hint and suggest and imply, but we don't confront.

"Will you at least consider calling Joel?" Dad asks. "He misses you. He told me so himself when we had lunch last week after his shift."

Of course they've been having lunch with Joel. Probably strategizing ways to bring me back to the fold.

"I talk to Joel almost every day about Alana," I say. "We're civil. That's the best I can offer right now."

Dad sighs, the sound heavy with disappointment. "You're making a mistake, Deborah."

"Maybe." I reach for my purse. "But it's my mistake to make."

The words hang in the air between us, unfamiliar and almost shocking in their defiance. I've never pushed back like this before. I've disagreed in small ways, made minor rebellions, but ultimately, I've always bent to their will, to their vision of who I should be.

Not anymore.

Mom follows me to the door, her steps quick and agitated. "We're having Shabbat dinner Friday. You'll bring Alana?" It's not really a question.

"I'll check with her. She might have plans." Another small rebellion—the suggestion that my daughter might have priorities that don't revolve around family obligations.

"What plans could be more important than Shabbat with her grandparents?"

I don't answer, just lean in to kiss her cheek. "I'll call you tomorrow."

Outside, the autumn air feels cleansing against my flushed skin. I sit in my car for a moment, hands gripping the steering wheel, taking deep breaths. The conversation replays in my head, but this time, I notice things I've always missed before: the way they tag-team their questions, the subtle redirections when I try to assert myself, the implied threats about what my choices mean for Alana.

How did I never see it before? The manipulation masked as concern, the control disguised as love.

I start the engine and pull away from their perfect house with its perfect landscaping.

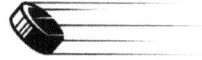

Inside, the rink is eerily quiet. My footsteps echo as I make my way toward the ice, where a single figure glides smoothly across the surface. Danny moves with such confidence on the sled that it's almost mesmerizing: his upper body powerful and controlled, the picks of his sticks biting into the ice with precision. He hasn't noticed me yet, and for a moment, I just watch.

"You planning on joining me, or just enjoying the view?" he calls out without looking my way.

I feel heat rise to my cheeks as I approach the entrance to the rink. "Just studying your technique. Know thy enemy and all that."

He turns the sled in a tight circle and pushes over to me, stopping with impressive precision. "Enemy, huh? And here I thought I was your coach." His beard can't hide his smile.

I hold out one of the coffee cups. "Peace offering."

"Smart tactical move." He takes a sip, then nods toward the bench where he's laid out equipment. "Ready to be humiliated again?"

"Such a motivational speaker," I say, but I'm already taking off my jacket. "I brought knee pads this time. And elbow pads. And honestly considered a helmet for walking around my house."

Danny laughs, the sound echoing off the high ceiling. "Preparation is half the battle. The other half is accepting that you're going to fall down. A lot."

"Encouraging."

"But," he adds, his tone softening, "you're going to get better every time."

Getting into the sled is slightly less awkward today. I know to brace myself as Danny helps lower me onto the seat. His hands are warm and sure as he adjusts the straps around my legs.

"Not too tight?" he asks, looking up at me.

I shake my head, suddenly aware of how close his face is to mine. "It's fine."

He wheels back slightly. "Yesterday you kept trying to use your feet to balance or move. It's instinct, I know, but—"

"But I need to stop," I finish for him. "I get it. Legs are dead weight in this game."

Something flickers across his face, so quickly I almost miss it. "Exactly," he says, his voice even. "Today we're focusing on core strength and balance. You need to feel the center of the sled."

For the next twenty minutes, Danny has me practicing just staying upright while stationary, then making small movements forward and backward. It's less embarrassing without an audience, and I find myself improving already.

"Good," he says when I manage to propel myself forward in a relatively straight line. "Now try turning."

I dig one stick pick into the ice a little harder than the other, and the sled begins to curve. "I'm doing it!" I exclaim, sounding like a child learning to ride a bike.

"Don't get cocky," Danny warns, but he's smiling. "Try the other direction."

I overcorrect, nearly tipping over, but catch myself. My arms are already burning with effort, unused to this particular kind of strain.

This is insane," I pant after another fifteen minutes of drills. "How do you make it look so effortless? You've been playing for years, right?"

Danny chuckles, his sled gliding in a smooth circle around me. "Actually, only a few months. Murph started the team back in September."

"Seriously?" I stop moving, nearly tipping over from the sudden halt. "But you're so good at it."

He shrugs, a gesture I remember from high school whenever anyone complimented him. "Upper body strength was always my thing, even before..." He trails off, gesturing vaguely at his legs. "And I picked it up pretty quick. Something about it just clicked for me."

"What do you like about it?" I ask, genuinely curious. "The sport, I mean."

Danny's quiet for a moment, considering. His eyes drift across the empty rink, taking in the expanse of ice gleaming under the fluorescent lights.

"The speed," he finally says. "There's a freedom to it. When I'm moving fast across the ice, it's like...everything else falls away." His voice softens. "And it's the team, too. There's something about being part of something, you know? We're all figuring it out together."

I nod, understanding completely. "I get that. I miss that feeling."

"What, being part of a team?"

"Being part of anything that's just for me," I admit. "Something that's not about being someone's wife or mother or daughter."

Our eyes meet, and for a moment, neither of us speaks. There's a recognition there, an understanding that transcends the years and choices that separated us.

"Well," he says finally, breaking the silence, "you're part of this now. For better or worse."

"Mostly worse, based on my performance," I laugh.

"You'll get there." He checks his watch. "We should probably wrap this up."

I glance at the clock on the wall, surprised at how quickly the hour has passed. "Same time tomorrow?"

"If you're up for it." Danny gets out of his sled first and from his wheelchair, leans forward to help me out of mine.

"I'll be sore as hell, but I'll be here," I promise.

As I stand, my legs wobble slightly, stiff from being immobilized and I grip his shoulder to keep from falling over. Danny looks up at me from his chair, and suddenly I'm aware of our reversed positions—me standing above him, unsteady on my feet, while he sits securely in his element.

"Thanks for doing this," I say, meaning it. "I know you didn't have to."

"Call it paying it forward," he replies. "Murph did the same for me when I started."

We gather our things in comfortable silence.

"See you tomorrow, coach," I call as we part ways at our cars.

Danny

The crack of sticks against the ice echoes through the rink as Deb races past Jack, swiping the puck away with a precision that wasn't there a week ago. I can't help the grin spreading across my face as she completes the drill without tipping over once. She catches my eye from across the rink and gives a little victorious nod, like she's saying, "See? Told you I could do it." I never doubted her for a second.

"Damn, Deb!" Robbie calls out as he glides up beside me. "You sure you haven't been secretly practicing in the middle of the night?"

She laughs, the sound bouncing off the high ceiling of the rink. "I never said I wasn't!"

We're only ten minutes into practice, but the difference in Deb from our first session is night and day. The extra one-on-one practices are paying off. She's still not great, but she's no longer a liability on the ice. In fact, she might actually help us win this thing.

"Alright, let's run the passing drill," Murph calls out, his voice carrying that coach-like authority that none of us question. "Mark and Robbie on defense, Deb and Jack on offense. Danny, you're with me in goal."

We settle into our positions, the scrape of metal blades against ice creating that rhythmic white noise that feels like home to me now. Deb and Jack exchange a look before she pushes forward, her movements more confident than even yesterday. She's a quick study, always has been.

"Don't go easy on her!" I shout to Mark, who grins and squares his shoulders.

The puck skitters across the ice as Jack makes a clean pass to Deb. She catches it on her stick blade—a move that would have sent her sprawling a week ago—and pivots, heading straight for Mark. He lunges to block her, but she fakes left, then pushes right, and suddenly she's clear with a shot on goal.

I brace myself, but her shot sails wide, missing the net by at least a foot.

"Crap!" She slams her stick against the ice in frustration.

"Hey, the fact that you got past Mark is huge," I call out. "The shot will come."

Jack slides over and bumps her sled gently with his. "That move was sick. If I'd been in position, I could've caught that rebound."

Deb's face brightens a bit at that. "Next time, I'll aim it at you instead of the goal."

"There's some strategy for you," Murph laughs. "Miss on purpose!"

We reset and run the drill again. And again. By the fourth attempt, Deb's arms are visibly shaking from exertion, but she's landing more passes, making cleaner moves. The whole team is clicking better than we ever have before.

"Water break," Murph calls out eventually, and we all head to the benches.

I pull up next to Deb, who's red-faced and breathing hard but looking more alive than I've seen her since she came back to Cedar Harbor.

"Not bad for an accountant," I tell her, passing her a water bottle.

"I think that's the nicest thing you've said since I moved back, Danny."

"Don't let it go to your head. You still skate like you're being chased by bees."

She splashes a bit of her water at me, and I dodge, laughing.

"Hey, Danny," Murph calls from across the rink. "Can you grab those new jerseys from the equipment room? Coach Simmons dropped them off yesterday."

I nod, already moving. "Sure thing."

It doesn't even occur to me to ask Deb to go instead, though she's sitting right there and could probably get there faster. It's just habit—I'm the guy who fetches things, who reaches high shelves, who carries equipment. The mobile one. There are times it makes me feel like I'm not part of either world. I'm too disabled for the able-bodied people and I'm too abled for the disabled community. I fit no where, belong no where.

I get out of my sled and into my wheelchair, pushing down the long hallway toward the equipment room, my shoulders already tensing at the prospect of what's waiting. The room is at the end of the corridor, past the locker rooms and through a heavy fire door that always sticks in the winter. I push through it with a grunt, the hinges protesting loudly.

Inside, the fluorescent lights flicker on to reveal walls lined with shelves and gear piled everywhere. It smells like rubber and sweat and disinfectant. The jerseys are probably in one of the upper lockers, because nothing in my life is ever easy.

Sure enough, I spot a box on the top shelf with "WHEELCHAIR MAFIA" scrawled across the side in Sharpie. I position my chair directly beneath it and reach up, my fingertips just brushing the cardboard. Not quite.

I put my feet on the floor, brace one hand on the shelf, and pull myself upward. Pain shoots through my back and into my legs—the nerves that still work firing off angry protests. But I've gotten good at ignoring pain. I stretch further, my fingers closing around the edge of the box.

Got it.

I ease it forward until gravity takes over, catching it against my chest as I settle back down. My legs are spasming now, little involuntary twitches that always follow when I push too hard. I wait for them to subside, breathing through the discomfort. No one needs to see this part.

By the time I wheel back onto the ice, jerseys in my lap, my face is composed again. The team whoops when they see the bright blue fabric.

"Looking sharp!" Jack calls out, grabbing one from the pile.

"These are way better than those ratty practice pinnies," Mark agrees, pulling his over his head.

Deb takes hers with a smile. "I get a real jersey? I feel official now."

"You earned it," Murph tells her.

I watch as the team sorts through sizes, joking and pulling them on over their pads. Deb's fits a bit loose, making her look smaller somehow, more vulnerable. But when she pushes back onto the ice, her movements are anything but fragile.

"Ready for Bedford next week?" Robbie asks her.

She nods, determination setting her jaw. "Ready as I'll ever be."

We spend the rest of practice running plays, working on positioning, fine-tuning the little details that will matter in a real game. When Murph finally calls an end to practice, we're all exhausted but buzzing with a kind of electric anticipation. This is really happening. We're going to play our first real game.

"Good work today, everyone," Murph says as we gather our gear. "We actually look like a team now."

"A winning team," Mark adds, his smile wide.

Deb catches up to me in the hallway, her hair damp with sweat at the temples, cheeks still flushed from exertion. "Thanks for all your help," she says. "I wouldn't be ready without those extra practices."

I shrug, uncomfortable with the gratitude. "You did the work."

"Still," she insists. "It means a lot."

I nod, not trusting myself to say more. Because the truth is, those extra practices have meant a lot to me too, in ways I'm not ready to examine too closely.

"See you tomorrow?" she asks, pausing at the women's locker room door.

"Same time, same place," I confirm, and watch as she disappears inside, already looking forward to it more than I should.

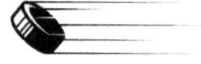

The clock on my microwave blinks 11:42 PM, but I'm still planted in my recliner, fighting to keep my eyes open through another episode of whatever reality show is playing. I've lost track of how many I've watched tonight. The TV casts blue shadows across my living room as gorgeous people with perfect teeth argue about nothing. Usually this mindless drama is the perfect way to unwind, but tonight my thoughts keep drifting back to the rink, to Deb's smile when she nailed that crossover move, to the way the past seems determined to collide with my present.

I reach for the remote and click to the next episode. Anything to postpone what's waiting for me when I close my eyes.

It wasn't always like this. Before Deb showed up at dinner, I slept like the dead. But now? Now the nights stretch endlessly, filled with fragments of memories I'd rather forget.

My phone buzzes on the side table. A text from Murph: "Got word from Bedford. Game's at 2pm, not 4. Can everyone make it?"

I thumb back a quick "Yes" and toss the phone aside. The team's excited about the game, and I should be too. Instead, I'm sitting here at nearly midnight, avoiding sleep like it's an enemy.

My walker sits beside the recliner, metal frame gleaming dully in the television light. I know I should haul myself to bed, take my meds, go through my stretches. Be responsible. But the thought of lying down, of surrendering to unconsciousness, makes my skin crawl.

On screen, someone throws a drink in someone else's face. I force myself to focus on their petty drama instead of the memories creeping at the edges of my mind. Memories of rain-slick asphalt. Of Deb's voice saying words that shattered everything I thought I knew about us.

I don't realize I've dozed off until I jerk awake, neck cramped at an awkward angle. The TV is showing a different program now—some late-night talk show with a host I don't recognize. I grab the remote and hit the power button, plunging the room into darkness.

No more stalling. I push myself upright, muscles protesting after hours in the same position. My calves are tight from today's practice, and my back throbs dully as I lean on the walker. I pause to wait out the tiny spasms racing up and down my calf muscles that make my legs too shaky to walk on. Finally I push forward, the hardwood floor creaking beneath me while I make my halting way down the hall toward the bedroom with my dramatic limp.

The nightly routine is automatic—brush teeth, wash face, strip to my boxers, catheter. In bed, I run through my stretches: ankles, calves, hamstrings. The motions are mechanical, my mind elsewhere. I wish I could text someone, anyone, just to keep myself awake a little longer. But who would answer at this hour? And what would I say? "Hey, can't sleep because I'm terrified of dreaming."

I switch off the lamp and lie back, staring at the ceiling. The familiar weight of dread settles over me like a blanket. Just get through the night, I tell myself. One more night. Even though after that it will be another "just one more night" and another and another. My brain can tell I'm lying to it, trying to trick it.

Sleep comes for me anyway, dragging me under despite my resistance.

At first, there's nothing—just the blessed emptiness of deep dreamless rest. Then slowly, insidiously, the images start to form. Rain falling in sheets. Streetlights reflecting in puddles. The smell of wet asphalt.

I'm walking—fully walking, no chair, no walker—along the railroad tracks that cross over historic Main Street. The metal ties are slippery beneath my boots. In the dream, I can feel every step, every impact of heel against steel. The sensation is so vivid it's almost painful, this memory of what it was like to move without thinking, without planning, without pain.

The night is dark except for the distant glow of town lights. I can see my breath clouding in front of me. My hands are numb with cold.

The dream stops following history and becomes disjointed— flashes of dark, cold, wet. There isn't real pain in the dream, just the memory of it.

I wake gasping, sheets twisted around my legs, sweat cold on my skin despite the chill in the room. My heart hammers against my ribs like it's trying to escape. I push myself upright, breathing hard, trying to orient myself in the present.

The digital clock on my nightstand reads 3:17 AM. Another night, another episode. I swing my legs over the side of the bed, feeling the familiar disconnect—my brain saying "stand" and my body responding with "maybe, sort of, if we're lucky." I reach for the water glass on the nightstand, hands shaking so badly I nearly spill it.

This has to stop. I can't keep reliving that night every time I close my eyes. But what's the alternative?

My legs ache with tingly nerve pain, a reminder of consequences that can never be undone. I press my fingers into the muscles, massaging gently, though it does little good.

I rub my eyes and reach for the light. Might as well get up. There's no rest for me here, not tonight.

Deborah

I scrape uneaten brisket into a Tupperware container, the familiar rhythm of my mother's kitchen clean-up as ingrained as my childhood prayers. The good china stacks with precise clinks—never in the dishwasher, always hand-washed, always dried immediately with the special embroidered towels. Some things in the Cohen household are eternal, unchanging since I was Alana's age.

Friday night dinner at my parents' house—another ritual preserved in amber. Mom still makes the same brisket recipe, still uses the same Shabbat candlesticks that belonged to my grandmother, still frets if anyone takes less than seconds. Dad still dominates the conversation with stories about his clients and golf games.

I rinse a serving platter under hot water, watching the pattern of blue flowers emerge from beneath gravy smears. My father's voice carries from the study where he's showing Alana his collection of legal books, a not-so-subtle hint about career paths he deems worthy. I can tell by the monosyllabic responses that she's being polite but uninterested.

The faucet squeaks when I turn it off—the same squeak it's had since I was in high school. I dry my hands and move to put away the leftovers, the refrigerator door opening with that same familiar suction sound.

Then my mother's voice drifts in from the hallway, lower than her dinner table voice but clear enough to carry. "She's in the kitchen. Come, I want to show you something."

I pause, hands still holding the Tupperware. Footsteps move away from the kitchen, toward the living room. I hear Alana's curious "What is it, Bubbe?" before they move out of earshot. I should keep cleaning, give them their privacy, but something in my mother's tone makes me set down the container and move closer to the doorway.

"—your mother's Harvard acceptance letter," my mother is saying as I approach. "We had it framed. Such a proud moment."

"I didn't know Mom went to Harvard," Alana says, surprise evident in her voice.

"Oh yes. Pre-law, though she switched to accounting later. Your grandfather and I worked very hard to keep her on track. She was always smart, but easily influenced. Especially by that boy."

My breath catches. That boy. Even thirty years later, she can't bring herself to say Danny's name.

I flatten myself against the wall beside the kitchen doorway, heart suddenly pounding. I should walk in there, change the subject, but my feet won't move.

"What boy?" Alana asks, her voice dropping to match my mother's conspiratorial tone.

"Just a local boy. A mechanic's son." The dismissal in my mother's voice stings even now. "He wanted her to stay in Cedar Harbor after high school. Can you imagine? All that potential, wasted on some small-town romance."

"Did she want to stay with him?" Alana asks, and I can hear the spark of interest in her voice.

"She thought she did." My mother's sigh is theatrical. "But she was eighteen, what did she know? It took a lot of...guidance...to help her see reason. Zayde and I, we prevented her from making a terrible mistake."

I close my eyes, feeling the weight of that "guidance" like it was yesterday. The tearful arguments, the silent treatments, the parade of "suitable" boys from good Jewish families invited to dinner. The pointed comments about Danny's prospects compared to Joel's medical school acceptance.

"Your father was such a catch," my mother continues. "A nice Jewish doctor from a good family. We knew he would give Deborah the kind of life she deserved. And look at you! Our beautiful granddaughter. Everything worked out just as it should."

Just as it should. The words echo in my mind as I stand frozen in the hallway. Did it, though? Did marrying Joel give me the life I deserved, or just the life my parents thought I should want?

"Mom doesn't seem very happy about how things worked out," Alana says softly.

"She's just going through a phase," my mother says dismissively. "Midlife crisis. She'll come to her senses eventually. The important thing is that we kept her from throwing away her future back then."

Throwing away my future. The phrase burns in my chest. Was that what choosing Danny would have been? Or would it have been choosing a different kind of future—one with less status and money, perhaps, but with the kind of love that makes your heart race even thirty years later?

I back away from the doorway, returning to the kitchen on unsteady legs. My hands tremble as I finish wrapping the leftovers, my thoughts spinning with the weight of what I just heard...and what Alana just heard.

She needs to hear my side of this story. That the choices I'm making now aren't impulsive or reckless; they're the result of decades of suppressing what I truly wanted.

I stack the last of the dishes in the cabinet and take a deep breath. The drive back to The Whispering Pines will give me time to think about what to say, how to explain the complicated web of expectations and obedience that led me to where I am now.

In the car, Alana is quiet, staring out the window at the passing streetlights. I can practically see the questions forming behind her eyes, but she doesn't ask them. Not yet. The silence between us feels weighted, filled with unspoken histories.

"That was...nice," she says finally, her tone making it clear it was anything but.

"They mean well," I say automatically, the response I've been giving my whole life when people notice my parents' controlling behavior.

"Do they?" Alana turns to look at me directly. "Bubbe showed me your old bedroom. It still has all your debate trophies and honor roll certificates. Like a shrine to the person they wanted you to be."

My grip tightens on the steering wheel. "They're proud of my accomplishments."

"They're proud of the things that fit their narrative," she corrects me, and I'm startled by her insight. "Not the same thing."

I stop at a light, watching it reflect red against the dashboard. My daughter is waiting for me to contradict her, to defend my parents as I always have. But I'm tired of the script, tired of pretending their vision for my life was the only right path.

"We need to talk," I say finally as the light turns green. "When we get back to our room. There are things about my life—about my choices—that I think you should understand."

She nods, a small smile playing at the corners of her mouth. "I'd like that."

The rest of the drive passes in silence, but it's different now, expectant rather than tense. For the first time, I feel ready to tell my daughter the truth about the road not taken, about the boy I left behind, about the small, quiet rebellion I'm finally allowing myself by moving back to Massachusetts. About how sometimes the biggest mistakes aren't the ones you make, but the ones you let others prevent you from making.

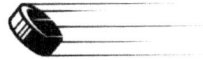

The Whispering Pines glows against the evening sky, its warm yellow windows a stark contrast to the cool formality of my parents' house. As Alana and I climb the porch steps, I feel the tension in my shoulders begin to ease. It's strange how quickly this place has become a sanctuary—somewhere I can breathe without feeling judged. Even the creaking floorboards under my feet seem to welcome me back, each groan and sigh of old wood telling stories of the countless people who've found temporary refuge here, just like us.

Inside, Alana heads for the stairs but pauses when Karen emerges from the small office behind the check-in desk, reading glasses perched on her nose and a mug of tea in hand.

"There you are!" Karen's smile is genuine, lacking the calculated warmth my mother reserves for social occasions. "How was dinner with the folks?"

"Predictable," I say, and Alana snorts beside me.

Karen laughs. "That good, huh? Well, I just put out some fresh cookies in the sitting room if you need something sweet to wash away the taste of family obligation."

"Thanks, but I'm stuffed with guilt-inducing brisket," I reply. "Rain check?"

"Always." She leans against the banister. "Oh, before I forget—I ran into Danny at the hardware store today. He was picking up supplies for your place. How's that coming along? When's moving day?"

The mention of Danny sends an unexpected flutter through my chest. I haven't told my parents that he's doing most of the renovation work. They'd probably have simultaneous heart attacks.

"It's coming along better than expected," I say, unable to keep the excitement from my voice. "The electrical is almost completely updated. Turns out it wasn't as bad as we thought. And the plumbing in the main bathroom is finished."

"That's fantastic!" Karen exclaims. "Those are usually the most troublesome."

"And expensive," I add. "Danny says we can start moving in whenever we're ready." I turn to Alana, who's been uncharacteristically quiet. "The kitchen will still be a work in progress, but everything else should be livable."

Alana nods. "Does that mean I'll have to eat takeout for dinner every night? Because I'm actually okay with that."

I laugh. "Don't get too excited. We'll have a microwave and a hot plate until the new appliances are installed. Danny's going to help me put up this gorgeous pale lavender paint I found."

"Purple," Alana corrects me with a smile. "You promised me purple."

"Lavender is a shade of purple," I counter.

"Barely," she says, but there's no real complaint in her tone. I've noticed her warming to the cottage more with each visit, especially since Danny installed the window seat in her room—a detail I remembered she admired during our first viewing.

"What else is on the renovation list?" Karen asks, settling into one of the armchairs in the lobby.

I sit across from her, eager to share. "The kitchen is the big one. We're taking it down to the studs next week. New cabinets, countertops, flooring—everything. I found these beautiful reclaimed wood shelves at that salvage place in Eastport."

"Open shelving?" Karen raises her eyebrows. "Bold choice."

"I've spent my whole adult life hiding my mismatched dishes behind cabinet doors," I say. "I'm ready for a little honesty in my kitchen."

Alana perches on the arm of my chair. "She's getting this huge farmhouse sink that could probably fit a small child."

"For washing big pots," I clarify quickly.

"Or hiding bodies," Alana adds with a straight face that makes Karen burst out laughing.

"The hardwood floors in the living room are being refinished the week after next," I continue. "They're actually in amazing shape under all those layers of carpet and linoleum. Danny says they're original to the house."

"That's one of the things I love about these old places," Karen says, gesturing around at the B&B. "They've got good bones. Just need someone who sees their potential."

"Exactly," I say, feeling a rush of vindication. My parents see only the cottage's flaws—the outdated fixtures, the small rooms, the quirky layout. But Karen understands what I see: possibilities, character, a canvas for creating the life I actually want.

"And are you still planning to commute to Boston for that accounting job?" Karen asks.

I shake my head. "No, actually. I got an offer from a firm in Arlington yesterday. It's a smaller office, but the work is interesting—local businesses, some nonprofit clients. And the best part is it's only fifteen minutes from the house."

"That's wonderful news!" Karen exclaims. "We should celebrate."

"Let's wait until we actually move in," I suggest. "Have a proper housewarming."

"Deal." Karen stands, sensing perhaps that Alana and I are ready to head upstairs. "Susan's making her famous French toast for breakfast tomorrow. Seven-thirty if you want it hot."

"We'll be there," I promise, rising from my chair.

As we climb the stairs to our room, I feel Alana watching me, that same thoughtful expression from the car ride still on her face.

I take a deep breath as we reach our door. It's time for truths long buried to finally see light.

Our room at The Whispering Pines feels impossibly small suddenly, like the walls themselves are pressing in to witness this confession. Alana sits cross-legged on the bed, her back against the headboard, scrolling through something on her phone but I can tell she's not really seeing it. She's waiting. I close the door behind us with a soft click and stand there for a moment, trying to gather words that have been buried for decades. How do you tell your fifteen-year-old daughter that you've been living a compromise? That her entire existence rests on a foundation of choices made out of fear rather than love?

The bedsprings creak as I sit beside her. Alana sets her phone down, giving me her full attention. In the soft lamplight, she looks so much like me at her age that it makes my chest ache.

"So," she says, breaking the silence, "who was 'that boy' Bubbe mentioned?"

I take a deep breath. "His name is Daniel."

"And Bubbe and Zayda hated him," she says.

"They didn't think he was suitable," I correct her, though she's not wrong. "Danny's father was a mechanic. They lived in a little Cape Cod on the outskirts of town. His mom left when he was young, so it was just the two of them. He worked in his dad's garage after school, fixing cars."

"So he was poor," Alana says flatly.

"They weren't poor, exactly. Just...working class. And not Jewish." I twist my fingers together in my lap. "My parents had very specific ideas about who I should end up with. A Jewish boy from a good family, college-bound, professional track."

"Like Dad."

"Exactly like your father." I stare down at my hands, seeing the faint indentation where my wedding ring used to sit. "When I got accepted to Harvard, Danny and I had a plan. I'd go to school in Boston, and he'd start trade school. He'd come visit on weekends. We'd make it work."

"What happened?" Alana asks softly.

I close my eyes briefly, the memories washing over me. "My parents happened. They...orchestrated things. They made it clear that if I stayed with Danny, I'd be cut off. No tuition help, no support. And they...they introduced me to Joel at a family friend's party that spring."

"They set you up with Dad?"

I nod. "Joel was perfect on paper. Pre-med at Harvard, from a prominent Jewish family in Newton. Our parents were thrilled. They pushed for us to spend time together, invited him to every family event."

"But you were still with Danny?"

"Yes." My voice catches. "I tried to balance both worlds for a while. But the pressure was relentless. Every day, some new comment from my mother about Danny's prospects, his background. Every day, some new praise for Joel's intelligence, his promising future."

I remember those suffocating months clearly—the growing sense that I was disappointing everyone, the constant guilt, the nagging fear that maybe my parents were right. Maybe Danny and I were too different to make it work.

"They kept saying I was too young to tie myself to my high school boyfriend, that I needed to explore options, that I'd regret limiting myself so early." I swallow hard. "They made it seem like choosing Danny would mean throwing away my future. Like I couldn't possibly have both love and success."

Alana's face is solemn. "So you broke up with him?"

"Prom night." My voice is barely audible now. "It was the hardest thing I'd ever done. He was so hurt, so confused. We'd been planning our future together for years and suddenly I was ending it."

"Because Bubbe and Zayda told you to?"

"Because I was eighteen and scared and didn't know how to stand up to them." I look directly at her now. "I let them convince me that practical considerations were more important than feelings. That security and status mattered more than happiness."

"And then you started dating Dad?"

I nod slowly. "Joel was there at Harvard, part of the same social circle. It was...easy. Comfortable. My parents were thrilled. His parents were thrilled. Everyone kept telling me how lucky I was, what a catch he was."

"But you didn't love him?" Alana's question is gentle, not accusing.

"I thought I could grow to love him. I thought love was something that developed from friendship and shared goals." I reach for her hand, needing her to understand. "I did care about your father, Alana. We built a life together. And he gave me you—the best thing that's ever happened to me."

She squeezes my hand but stays quiet, waiting for me to continue.

"The thing is," I say, my voice growing stronger, "I followed all the rules. I made the sensible choice. I married the right kind of man, moved to the right neighborhood, joined the right synagogue, had the right kind of career. I did everything my parents wanted. And none of it made me happy."

"Is that why you and Dad split up?"

"Part of it. We'd been drifting apart for years. The divorce was mutual—we both recognized we were living separate lives under the same roof." I take a shaky breath. "But coming back here, seeing Danny again...it's made me realize something I've been trying to ignore for thirty years."

Her eyes are fixed on mine, so open, so accepting.

"I regret every single day that I didn't choose love," I whisper, the admission finally breaking free. "I regret letting my parents' outdated rules dictate my happiness. I regret not being brave enough to follow my heart."

"This is the shop teacher, isn't it?"

"What? You have a shop class?"

"Yeah. Mr. Wallace. Gruff old guy in a wheelchair."

"He's the same age as me."

She raises her eyebrows as if to say, "So?"

"Yes, Danny Wallace. That's him," I say. "You like him?"

"He's a great teacher," she says. "Seems like a good dude."

"He's not the same boy I knew. I'm not the same girl. We've both lived whole lives apart."

"But you still care about him," she says, not a question.

"Mostly I care about teaching you to make choices based on what truly matters to you, not what others expect."

Alana's quiet for a moment, absorbing everything. Then she says, "I always thought there was something off about you and Dad. Like you were roommates, not people in love."

"You could tell?"

She nods. "Dad was always more interested in his medical journals than in talking to you. And you never looked at him the way Karen looks at Susan—like seeing them is the best part of your day."

The observation stuns me. How had my teenage daughter seen so clearly what took me decades to acknowledge?

"Plus," she continues with a mischievous glint in her eye, "this is way more interesting than I thought. My mom had a forbidden romance with the shop teacher? That's practically a movie plot."

I laugh but I'm still feeling guilty that I disrupted her life so much, made her move to a new school as a teen, left her father, changed her home, everything. I ask, "Tell me the truth, do you wish I had stayed with Dad? I know all of this is hard on you."

"Nah. I'd rather have a mom who's finally doing what makes her happy."

Her words fill me with a validation I didn't know I needed. I squeeze her hand, tears pricking the corners of my eyes. "How did you get so wise?"

"Must be those Cohen genes Bubbe's always going on about," she says with a smirk.

We sit in comfortable silence for a moment, the weight of secrets finally lifted. Then Alana asks, "So what happens now? With Mr. Wallace, I mean."

"I don't know," I admit. "We're just...finding our way back to friendship. Anything more is complicated."

"Because of the wheelchair?" she asks bluntly.

"No," I say immediately, surprised by the question. "Because we're different people now. Because there's history and hurt between us. Because I'm not sure either of us is ready."

She nods, considering this. "But you're open to possibilities?"

The question makes me smile. Am I open to possibilities? After decades of living within carefully constructed boundaries, the idea of possibilities feels revolutionary.

"Yes," I tell her, feeling the truth of it settle in my bones. "I'm open to possibilities."

Alana's smile widens. She leans forward and hugs me, a real hug, not the quick obligatory one she usually offers. "Good," she whispers against my shoulder. "Because I think he still looks at you the way Karen looks at Susan."

I hold my daughter close, this miraculous person who sees more clearly than I ever gave her credit for. Outside our window, the pines whisper in the evening breeze, their ancient voices seeming to affirm that it's never too late to find your way home.

Danny

The locker room smells like anticipation and nervous sweat. I adjust the straps on my sled hockey gear, watching my teammates do the same with varying levels of confidence. Mark's fingers fumble with his helmet while Jack methodically tightens each strap with the precision of someone who plans to avoid chaos through perfect preparation. Murph sits in the middle, our captain and coach all in one, his face set in determined lines. And Deborah sits in the corner, adjusting her borrowed gear, looking both terrified and exhilarated. Two weeks of training for her and four months for the rest of us, leading up to this moment—our first real game as the Cedar Harbor Sled Hockey team.

"Remember," Murph says, his voice steady and low, "we're here to play our game. Not theirs." He looks each of us in the eye, lingering on Deborah. "Play smart. Play together."

I wheel over to Deb while the others continue their preparations. "You ready for this?" I ask quietly.

She looks up, her hair pulled back in a tight ponytail, cheeks already flushed. "As ready as I'll ever be. Thanks to you. I won't let you guys down."

"Just remember, stay low in the sled and use your core like we practiced." I glance around to make sure no one's listening. "And if anyone asks—"

"Incomplete spinal cord injury from a car accident two years ago," she finishes with a half-smile. "I've got my cover story down pat."

The buzzer sounds, calling us to the ice. We file out of the locker room, the familiar scrape of wheels against concrete giving way to the hollow echo of the corridor leading to the rink. I take a deep breath, feeling that old pre-game tension—a sensation I haven't experienced since high school.

We emerge onto the ice to scattered applause. The stands aren't full, but they're not empty either. I spot Karen and Susan right away, waving a handmade banner that reads "GO CEDAR HARBOR!" in blue and white.

Next to them sits Alana, looking equal parts embarrassed and proud. Carly and Samantha are a few rows up, arms linked, while Becca sits beside them with intense focus, like she's studying for a test on hockey fandom. Even Kathleen from the Steamy Bean is here, her locs piled high, cheering loudly enough to compensate for ten people.

The Bedford team is already warming up on their end, their movements fluid and practiced. They've clearly been playing together for years.

"Don't look so terrified," Robbie says as he glides past me, his face bright with excitement. "We've got this."

Mark pushes himself into our warm-up circle, his movements still a bit hesitant but determined. "Do you think my mom's watching?" he asks, eyes scanning the stands.

"Front row," I tell him, nodding toward where his mother sits, clutching a program like it's a lifeline. "Looking proud already."

The referees signal for captains, and Murph pushes out to center ice. He looks tiny compared to Bedford's captain, but there's nothing small about the way he carries himself. They shake hands, exchange words I can't hear, and then we're lining up for the opening face-off.

I take my position on defense, the hard plastic of the sled secure beneath me. Across the ice, the Bedford defense eyes us with skepticism. I get it—we're the new guys, the unknowns. Probably an easy win in their minds. But they don't know what we've put into this.

The referee drops the puck. The game begins.

The first few minutes are a blur of motion and noise. Bedford gains possession immediately, their forwards charging toward our end with precision. Murph barks orders, positioning us to block their advance. I focus on the puck, on the angles, on keeping my sled between their forwards and our goal.

Jack, surprisingly, is the first to settle into rhythm. All those months of frustration at being new to disability, new to sports—it transforms into a fierce focus. He steals the puck from a Bedford forward with a precise movement of his stick, then passes it cleanly to Robbie.

"On your right!" I shout as a Bedford player charges Robbie's flank.

Robbie pivots, a move we've practiced for weeks, and passes to Deborah. She receives it, wobbling slightly but keeping control—a far cry from her first chaotic day on the ice. The training sessions have paid off. She pushes forward, managing a decent shot on goal that the Bedford goalie blocks easily, but it's a start.

The crowd erupts in encouraging cheers. I hear Alana's voice cutting through: "Go Mom!"

The first period continues with Bedford controlling the puck more often than not, but we hold our own defensively. Mark, our youngest, surprises me with his positioning. What he lacks in strength and speed, he makes up for in heart, throwing his small frame between the puck and our goal whenever needed.

By the second period, something shifts. We're finding each other on the ice more easily, anticipating movements, playing less as individuals and more as a unit. Murph's leadership is evident in every play—he's everywhere, directing traffic, supporting, encouraging.

Seven minutes into the second period, Robbie manages to steal the puck at center ice. He races toward Bedford's goal with surprising speed, his arms propelling his sled forward in bursts. Their defense converges on him, but at the last second, he passes to Jack who's positioned at the side of the goal.

Jack doesn't hesitate. His shot is clean and precise, sliding past the goalie's outstretched stick.

"Score!" The announcer's voice booms across the arena. "Cedar Harbor, one-zero!"

Our side of the stands erupts. I push over to Jack, my gloved hand clasping his shoulder. His face is a mix of shock and joy.

"Did I just—"

"First goal in team history," I confirm, grinning. "It's all you."

Bedford answers back quickly, their experience showing as they coordinate a series of passes that leaves our defense scrambling. They score, tying the game at one apiece. Murph just nods, unfazed. "Next point's ours," he tells us during a break.

The third period is when everything intensifies. Bedford scores again, putting them ahead. I can see frustration building in our team's faces, but also determination. No one's giving up.

Deborah catches my eye from her position. I nod encouragement. She's holding her own, moving better on the ice than anyone would expect. Our hours of extra practice are evident in her form, in the way she positions her body.

With five minutes left, Murph manages a beautiful goal on a power play, tying the score at two-all. The crowd is on their feet now, Karen and Susan leading the cheers.

The final minutes are a test of endurance. My arms burn from the constant pushing, from maneuvering the sled and handling the stick. But there's a clarity to the pain, a purpose.

With just over a minute left, Bedford makes a mistake. Their forward overcommits, leaving an opening. Mark, of all people, intercepts the puck. He hesitates for just a heartbeat, then pushes it toward Deborah who's in the clear.

She receives it cleanly, her face a mask of concentration. I hold my breath as she pushes toward the goal, the Bedford defense closing in. She doesn't try anything fancy—just a simple, direct shot, exactly as we practiced.

The puck slides past the goalie's stick and into the net just as her sled tips over, dumping her onto the ice. The buzzer sounds almost immediately after, marking the end of the game. Cedar Harbor: 3, Bedford: 2.

For a moment, I can't move. Then Mark crashes into me, his sled bumping mine as he throws his arms around my shoulders. "We won! We won!" he shouts, his voice cracking with emotion.

The rest of the team converges in a tangle of sleds and arms and laughter. Murph's usual stoic expression has given way to a grin that makes him look years younger. Jack looks stunned, like he can't quite believe what just happened. Robbie's already scanning the stands for Sam's reaction.

And Deborah—Deborah is radiant. She's gotten upright again and her face is flushed with exertion and joy, her eyes seeking mine across our celebrating teammates. When our gazes lock, there's something there I haven't seen in thirty years. Something that makes my heart race in a way that has nothing to do with the game we just played.

The audience spills onto the ice, surrounding us with congratulations and hugs.

As Alana wraps her arms around her mother, I watch them together, feeling something both warm and painful unfold in my chest. The bittersweet recognition of roads not taken, and the strange, unexpected ways they some-times circle back into view.

"Not bad for a rookie," I tell Deb when she finally makes her way to me, Murph's championship game puck clutched in her gloved hand.

"Had a good coach," she answers, her smile equal parts shy and bold. "Though I'm pretty sure I'll be nothing but bruises tomorrow."

"Worth it?" I ask, suddenly needing to know.

She looks around at our celebrating team, at her daughter chatting animatedly with Mark's mother, at the community that's embraced us both in different ways. Then her eyes return to mine.

"Every minute," she says softly. "Every single minute."

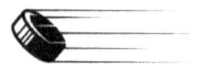

Kathleen's café is bursting with more noise than it's probably seen in years. Our team has taken over the largest table, and supporters spill onto surrounding ones, creating an island of celebration in the middle of Steamy Beans. Jack keeps reliving his goal, his hands moving in increasingly elaborate recreations while Becca watches him with bemused patience. Mark hasn't stopped smiling for a single second, his face practically glowing as his mother shows everyone the photos she took. Even Murph seems lighter somehow, as if the win has physically lifted weight from his shoulders.

"Next round's on me!" Karen announces, as Kathleen brings another tray of hot chocolate and coffee.

I sit back in my chair, content to watch rather than participate in the loud retelling of every play. My body aches in the best possible way—the satisfying fatigue of effort well spent. Across the table, Deborah is animated in a way I haven't seen since we were teenagers, laughing as Robbie dramatizes her game-winning shot.

"It was like slow motion," he insists, stretching his arms wide while his fingers remain curled up into his palms. "The puck just floated across the ice, and their goalie looked like he was moving through molasses."

"It wasn't nearly that graceful," Deb protests, but her smile betrays her pleasure.

"Mom, I got it all on video," Alana says, leaning over to show her phone. "I can't believe you actually scored the winning goal."

"Neither can I," Deb admits, catching my eye briefly across the table. There's something in her look that makes me glance away, suddenly very interested in the remaining crumbs of my chocolate chip cookie.

The celebration continues as the evening stretches on. Carly and Murph huddle together in a corner, their heads bent close as she shows him something on her phone. Sam sits perched on the arm of Robbie's chair, her hand resting lightly on his shoulder. The café gradually empties of other customers until it's just our group, loud and happy in the warmth of Kathleen's hospitality.

"We should do this after every game," Mark says, his usual shyness overcome by excitement.

"Bold of you to assume we'll win every game," Jack replies, but there's no edge to his words.

"We might not win every game," Murph says, rejoining the main conversation, "but we'll definitely celebrate every time we play. Win or lose."

This prompts a round of agreement and another toast with our mugs of now-lukewarm drinks. I notice Deb watching me over the rim of her cup, her eyes thoughtful.

When I catch her looking, she doesn't glance away like I did earlier.

As the night wears on, people begin to drift away. Mark's mother checks her watch and announces it's past bedtime. Karen and Susan leave to check on a guest who's arriving late. Carly and Murph head out together, followed shortly by Jack and Becca. Robbie and Sam linger a bit longer before saying their goodbyes.

"Need a ride, Mom?" Alana asks, gathering her coat. "I'm going with Robbie and Sam to drop some stuff at their place first."

Deb hesitates, looking from her daughter to me. "Actually, I think I'll stay a bit longer. Danny can give me a ride home, right?"

I nod, ignoring the flutter in my stomach. "Sure, no problem."

Alana looks between us, an unreadable expression crossing her face. Then she shrugs. "Okay, see you at home."

Soon it's just Deb, Kathleen, and me left in the café. Kathleen busies herself cleaning up, giving us space without making it obvious.

"I should probably get going," I say finally, when the silence between us stretches a bit too long. "It's been a long day."

"A good day," Deb corrects, standing and reaching for her coat.

I wheel toward the door, calling a thank you to Kathleen.

Outside, the night air is crisp and clean. Stars prick the darkness above us, unusually bright for a town with streetlights. We make our way to my truck in comfortable silence.

"I still can't believe we won," Deb says as I transfer throw my wheelchair into the bed and hobble back to the driver's seat. "I keep thinking I'm going to wake up and find out it was all a dream."

I start the engine, letting it warm up before pulling out. "You earned it. You worked harder than anyone these past couple weeks."

The drive to her cottage is short. The windows of the little house glow with welcoming light—Alana must have turned them on before leaving with Sam and Robbie. I pull into the driveway and shift into park.

"Want to come in?" Deb asks, her voice casual but her eyes intent. "I think there's still some of that wine left from last week. There's no ramp but..."

I hesitate, knowing I should say no, but nodding anyway. "I can manage the stairs."

I turn off the truck and we both get out. She looks away as I limp to the back to get my chair out and wheel over.

I line up my chair parallel to the three wooden steps and lock the brakes with a familiar click. My boots make contact with the frozen ground, the rubber soles crunching against crystalline snow. The metal railing bites into my palm like a strip of ice as I pull myself upright, my quadriceps and lower back muscles tensing like guitar strings as my weight shifts forward onto my toes. One hand grips the frost-slick metal, the other clutches my rigid titanium chair frame.

First step. Good. The weathered wood creaks beneath my weight.

Second step—my right calf seizes with a hot knife of pain. My left foot misses the lip of the stair and the railing wrenches away from my fingers.

The fall happens too fast for me to react—a sickening moment of weightlessness followed by impact. My body hits the ground hard, hip bone cracking against the edge of the bottom step, and the impact reverberates through me like a struck bell. The collision knocks the air from my lungs in a violent whoosh. Stars dance across my vision, silver pinpricks against sudden darkness. Cold seeps through my jeans, an immediate, biting chill on the backs of my legs that makes my damaged nerves fire in confused patterns.

"Danny!" Deb's face appears above me, her breath making clouds in the night air. Her hand hovers over my shoulder, uncertain. "God, are you—" Her eyes search mine, wide and full of worry.

"Just give me a second," I mutter, eyes fixed on the dark stain spreading across my knee where snow melts into denim. I push up on my elbows, but my body betrays me. My right leg twitches, heel digging a small trench in the snow.

Deb doesn't move for a moment. Then, slowly, she lowers herself to her knees beside me. The snow crunches loudly beneath her weight, and I hear the faint rustle of her jacket as she shifts closer. Her arm slides around my shoulders, steady and warm.

"Here," she says, her voice soft but firm.

The old me would have hated this: sprawled out on the lawn, pride in tatters, helpless as a turtle on its back while a woman hovered over me and tried to make gentle conversation out of humiliation. But that version of Danny Wallace fell behind somewhere. Maybe he never survived those first months in the hospital, when even sitting upright was an Olympic event and the world suddenly became a minefield of curbs, stairs, and other people's discomfort. Still, I feel the old frustration twitch in my gut as Deb's hand lightly brushes the snow from my beard. She shouldn't have to see me like this. I shouldn't have to let her.

"You don't have to—" I start to say, but her hand settles over mine, firm enough that the rest of the sentence withers in my mouth.

"*You* don't have to be strong all of the time," she says, each word landing with the finality of a period. She smooths the hair back from my temple, fingertips grazing the scar there, the one I always forget about until someone stares at it. "It's okay to let people help you."

She let's that sink in and I wonder why it's so difficult to accept. I've never wanted to give any leeway to my disability but sometimes I don't have a choice.

"Do you remember Mrs. Calloway?" she says.

I'm confused by the random question but yes, I remember her. Her husband died and she needed someone to clear out her gutters. "Yes," I say cautiously.

"You were over there every weekend helping her with all sorts of tasks."

"Someone had to do it."

"And that someone was always you. I admired that about you, how even as a kid you were so quick to help anyone and everyone. I didn't notice how you never let anyone take care of you."

"I didn't need taking care of," I say automatically.

"Everyone does sometimes. You don't have to give and give and give without ever getting anything back." Her eyes don't leave mine. She knows she's got my number. I swallow hard.

"You don't know what it's like," I say quietly, "Having to prove yourself worthy of the air you breathe every second of every day."

"Danny," she says softly, "your worth was never in question. Not to anyone who really knows you."

"Easy to say now," I mutter. "You didn't see me in those first years."

"No," she agrees. "I didn't. And I'm sorry for that."

That simple apology stops my breath for a moment. It feels good to know that she wishes she had been there for me in that dark time. After a long quiet moment she says, "Are you hurt?"

"Just my pride," I admit. "That and my ass. Maybe my hip if I'm lucky."

The cold is really biting now, creeping up my legs, and I can feel the ache setting in for tomorrow. I shift and grit my teeth, determined to salvage some dignity by trying again. I grab the railing, bracing for the pain that'll shoot up my hamstring, and Deb tightens her grip on my hand.

"We'll do it together," she says, like it's obvious.

I glance up at the porch light, the way it throws her features into a warm halo. There's an unspoken challenge there, and I recognize it as the same one that used to get us into trouble all over town: bet you can't. Bet you won't.

"Okay," I say, the word almost a dare. "Let's do it."

She braces her foot against the bottom stair for leverage, then her arm becomes a bridge under mine, warmth seeping through my jacket. We stay like that for a second, our ragged breaths fogging between us, both of us knowing this is going to suck and neither willing to be the first to say it. The cold drills through my jeans but her palm feels hot, almost feverish, in my grip.

"Ready?" she asks.

I nod, and together we heave. My center of gravity tilts precariously; for a split second I'm convinced I'm going to pull her down onto the ice with me. But Deb is stronger than she looks. She leans back, using her whole body to counterweight me, and somehow, I stagger upright, boots scraping for traction, the left one wobbling dangerously before finding its footing. My calf cramps hard but I bite down and push.

"Almost there," she grunts, her shoulder wedged under my armpit now, and we start inching up the steps. It's not elegant—more like an injured moose being dragged from a snowbank than any kind of coordinated effort—but we get one foot planted, then the next, my toe digging into the gritty ice. She doesn't let go for a second.

Halfway up, my vision pulses black at the edges and I get so dizzy my head feels like a boulder pulling me downward. Deb pauses, lets me breathe, then gives another tug.

"There we go," she whispers, more to herself than me.

At the top landing we collapse together, me slumping onto the porch bench and her crouching beside me, both of us panting. The adrenaline shakes start in my fingers, then travel up my arms and set my teeth chattering.

"You okay?" she asks, her face right next to mine.

"Yeah," I say, forcing a smile. "Been through worse."

She laughs, loud and shaky, and for a second, neither of us moves. I realize we're still holding hands, her thumb tracing idle circles across my skin.

"I'll get your chair," she whispers. She hops back down the stairs like it's nothing—for her, it is. The metal frame of my chair glints under the porch light as she drags it up, one bump at a time. I stumble my way from the bench to collapse onto the seat, the familiar give of the cushion an instant relief. She positions herself behind me and helps lever me over the threshold into the house, the door frame scraping my elbow as we cross.

Her cottage has transformed since I first assessed it for repairs. What was empty and echoing is now filled with furniture, rugs, and personal touches that make it unmistakably hers. Photos of Alana line the mantel, alongside books and small treasures that speak of a life I wasn't part of. The warmth feels like heaven and I'm glad we got that electrical taken care of.

"Let me grab you some dry clothes," she says. "I've got sweats that'll work."

Her footsteps fade down the hallway and she returns with a bundle of gray fabric. "These should fit."

Thankfully, she disappears into the kitchen to give me privacy to change. It takes a goddamn eternity to coax my uncooperative legs out of the jeans. The wet fabric clings stubbornly to my calves, and I have to stop twice to work through a muscle spasm in my right thigh.

I kick off my boots and finish working the jeans off, then scoot and shift until I'm balanced on the edge of the wheelchair cushion, naked from the waist down except for my boxers, which are also unfortunately soaked. My legs dangle uselessly while I size up the next challenge: sweatpants. The ones Deb brought are probably Alana's but my legs are smaller than they used to be despite how much work I put them through so the pants will fit.

Getting them on is a slow-motion wrestling match against my own limbs. Every tug sets off a cascade of little aftershocks from the fall—tiny pinpricks along my shins, a persistent ache behind my knee, and the dull throb of a bruised hip.

By the time I've wrangled the pants into place and tugged the waistband over my hips, I'm breathing hard and my skin is slick with sweat. I shove the damp jeans into a heap beside me and rest my elbows on my knees, letting my head hang for a second. The house is quiet. I can hear Deb moving around in the kitchen, running water and opening cabinets, letting me have this moment of private defeat.

I finally push up and reposition myself next to the sofa. My arms feel like noodles but at least the clothes are soft and dry.

Deb appears in the doorway holding two mugs of something steaming, her eyes softening when she sees me. She hands me a mug of hot chocolate, then settles on the couch. I remain in my chair, keeping a safe distance that feels necessary though I can't quite articulate why.

"To new beginnings," she says, raising her mug.

"To good teammates," I counter, clinking my mug against hers.

She takes a sip, her eyes never leaving mine over the rim. "I've been thinking about us a lot lately."

The words hang in the air between us. My heart picks up speed, treacherous in its hope. "Deb—"

"No, let me finish," she interrupts gently. "Coming back here, seeing you again...it's made me wonder what might have been. What could still be."

She sets her hot chocolate down and moves closer, her hand coming to rest lightly on my arm. The contact sends electricity through me, a reminder of feelings I thought I'd buried decades ago.

"We're not kids anymore," she continues, her voice soft. "We've lived whole lives apart. But being around you these past weeks, working together, laughing toge ther...it feels like coming home."

Before I can respond, she leans in, her intention clear in the tilt of her head, the softness in her eyes. For a moment, I'm seventeen again, and she's everything I ever wanted.

But I'm not seventeen. And memory is a powerful thing.

I pull back, creating space between us. "I can't."

Hurt flashes across her face. "Danny—"

"I gave everything back then," I say, the words coming out rougher than I intend. "You always held back, but I was all in. I can't do that again."

She sits back, confusion replacing hurt. "That was thirty years ago. We were practically children."

"And you chose a future that didn't include me," I say, the old pain surprising me with its sharpness. "Which was your right. But I can't just pretend that never happened."

"I'm not asking you to pretend," she says, her voice rising slightly. "I'm saying we're different people now. We could start fresh."

I shake my head, wheeling back a few inches. "There's no such thing as a clean slate, Deb. Not with us."

"So what, that's it? We can never move forward because of choices we made as teenagers?"

"It's not that simple." I run a hand through my hair. I should tell her the truth about what I did. But I can't. The words stick in my throat. "I liked having you on the team. I like being your friend. But anything more...I just can't risk it."

She's quiet for a long moment, studying my face. "You're scared," she finally says, not unkindly.

"Of course I am."

She nods, her lips pressed together and then I see in her face as she lets it go. "You should stay the night," she says. "Rest up from that fall. There's a spare room here on the first floor."

"Wish I could, but there's medications I need at home so I have to get back."

"Oh. I see. Well, I'm helping you back down the stairs, no arguments!"

I have to smile then. And I am honestly grateful, my body has had more than enough for one day and I wasn't exactly looking forward to getting the dry pants wet by scooting down the stairs on my butt.

Deb opens the front door and the night air rushes in, even colder now after being inside the warmth of her cottage. Deb steps out onto the porch ahead of me, her breath clouding in the frosty air. I wheel over to the door and bump down the threshold onto the porch.

"How should we do this?" she asks. "Do you want to lean on me?"

"I'll stay in the chair and go backwards if you can hold onto the back and control the descent." Then I add, "Always safer if I go down facing uphill."

"Oh great, a vote of confidence."

I chuckle and turn the chair so my back is to the stairs.

"Stand below me on the steps," I instruct, and I pull up into a wheelie position, leaning forward for balance, and reach one hand for the railing.

She moves into position..

"Ready?" she asks.

"Ready as I'll ever be."

I feel Deb's hands on the top of the rigid low back of my wheelchair and the weight of her body ready to absorb the impact of the bounce down each step.

"On three," I say. "One, two, three—"

I bump down the first step with one hand on the railing and the other on my pushrim, Deb controlling the chair from behind. Her body braces against the weight, feet planted firmly on the step below. We pause, both catching our breath.

"You okay?" I ask, twisting to see her face.

"I'm fine. You're the one doing all the work." She adjusts her grip. "Ready for the next one?"

We repeat the process for the second step, my arms straining to control the descent. The metal frame of my chair shudders slightly as we navigate the drop, but Deb holds firm, her stance wide and secure.

"Last one," she says, voice tight with concentration.

The final step is always the trickiest. I lower myself down, feeling every muscle in my back and shoulders protest. Deb's breathing is heavy behind me, but her hands never waver as she guides the chair onto level ground.

"We did it," she says, a note of triumph in her voice.

I release my death grip on the railing and pushrim, flexing my fingers to restore circulation. "Thanks."

"Any time," she says, her smile warm and kind. I have the strangest urge right then to kiss her but I push it aside.

She walks beside me as I wheel across the snowy yard toward my truck. The wheels crunch through the thin layer of ice on top of the snow, leaving parallel tracks behind us. Above, stars prick the darkness, impossibly bright and clear.

"I'll get your jeans," she says suddenly, turning back toward the house.

"Don't worry about it," I call after her. "I've got plenty."

But she's already jogging back up the steps, disappearing inside. I continue to my truck and decide while I'm accepting help, I'll just go all in. I climb up into the seat and wait for Deb to return with my wet jeans in a plastic bag.

"Could you throw the wheelchair into the back for me?" I say.

"Sure thing, but I'm not sure 'throw' is the word I would use." She pushes the empty chair to the back of the truck and I watch in the side mirror as she gingerly tries to get it up into the bed with the wheels still turning and fighting her. Before I can tell her to put the brakes on, though, she's got it in.

"Text me when you get home," she says, handing me the bag through the open window. "So I know you made it safely."

The concern in her voice catches me off guard. It's been a long time since anyone worried about me making it home. "I will," I promise.

She steps back, hugging herself against the cold. I start the engine, the truck rumbling to life beneath me. The headlights illuminate her standing there in her driveway, snowflakes beginning to drift down around her.

For a moment, I consider rolling down the window again, calling out something more—an apology, an explanation, something to soften the rejection from earlier. But what would I say? That I'm still haunted by everything that happened between us? That every time I look at her, I remember both the best and worst moments of my life?

Instead, I raise my hand in a small wave. She waves back, her smile visible even in the dim light.

As I pull away, I watch her in the rearview mirror, standing in the falling snow, growing smaller until she disappears from view.

The drive home is a blur, my hands gripping the steering wheel so tight my knuckles ache. I try to focus on the road, on the rhythm of the wipers against a light mist that's begun to fall, but my mind keeps slipping backward. Back to a different kind of rain on a different spring night, when I wore a rented tux with a blue carnation that matched Deb's dress, and thought the future was something you could hold in your hand like a promise.

The gymnasium smells like hair spray and punch and too many bodies in a small space. The decorations committee has transformed it into their version of "A Night to Remember," with silver streamers and paper stars hanging from the basketball hoops. The music is too loud, some pop song that everyone but me seems to know the words to. I don't care. I'm only here for Deb.

She looks beautiful in her blue dress with the thin straps that show off her shoulders. Her hair is different—curled and pinned up with little wisps framing her face. When she smiles at me, it's like being punched in the chest in the best possible way. I can't believe she's here with me. Can't believe she's mine.

Except something's off. Has been all night. Her smile doesn't quite reach her eyes. She keeps checking the clock on the wall, keeps glancing toward the door. When we dance, her body is stiff against mine, her mind some-where else entirely.

"Everything okay?" I ask during a slow song, my mouth close to her ear to be heard over the music.

"Fine," she says, but her eyes slide away from mine. "Just tired."

I don't push it. Maybe she's nervous about af-ter-prom, about the hotel room my friend Mike's older brother booked for us. We've talked about it—taking that step—but always in hypotheticals, in somedays. Maybe tonight is too real, too soon. I'd tell her we don't have to, that we can just go to the diner with everyone else, but I don't want to bring it up here, don't want to embarrass her.

Another song ends, and she steps back from me. "I need some air," she says, already turning away. "I'll be right back."

I wait by the punch bowl, watching the minutes tick by. Five. Ten. I ask Melissa if she's seen Deb in the bathroom. She hasn't.

I find her in the stairwell, sitting on the bottom step with her arms wrapped around her knees. The blue dress puddles around her like spilled water. She doesn't look up when I sit beside her.

"Some party, huh?" I try for lightness. "I think Coach Wilson just tried to breakdance."

She doesn't laugh. "Danny, we need to talk."

The words land like stones in my stomach. "About what?"

She takes a deep breath. "About the future. Our future."

"Okay." I reach for her hand, but she pulls it back, tucking it under her leg. "What about it?"

"I got my acceptance letter from Harvard yesterday."

"That's great!" I mean it. She's worked so hard, spent so many late nights studying. "I'm proud of you."

"I don't know how to say this," she continues. She bites the inside of her cheek as she does when she's nervous. Her pale pink lips are slick with some kind of lipstick and I long to lean just an inch forward and kiss her. Instead, I wait for what she's trying to tell me. She swallows hard. "These last few years with you have been magical. Like living in a fairy tale where the real world pressures don't matter and love overcomes everything."

My stomach tightens and I think of seeing her and Joel coming out of synagogue looking so perfect together, like they belonged to the same bedroom set. "It does if you want it to," I say finally. How many times had we told each other that nothing in the world mattered outside of our love for each other?

"It's too much," she says. "We're too different."

"You and me? We're too different?" The pitch of my voice jumps and I try to regain control of myself.

"We come from such different worlds, Danny, and there are different expectations for us. This has been a dream but it's time to wake up now. There's no future for us."

I skitter suddenly to my feet, panicked energy jumping all through my body.

"What future do you want, Deb? Any future it is, I'll give it to you. I don't care what it takes. Name what you want and I will make it happen."

"Oh, Danny," she says softly.

"No," I say, desperate to stop her, as though stopping her from speaking will stop it from happening. "No, no no. We've made plans. We've made promises. We are going to make it work."

The music from down the hall teases me in the following silence, speaking of a gushing love too sickly sweet to be real. In that moment I knew the truth...Deb was choosing Joel. The man her father liked. He would become a doctor, provide for her, give her Jewish babies. She would fit into the society she was raised to be in.

And me? I'd be a relic, a discarded plaything, an interesting story from her past. Her society friends will laugh that she was once so rebellious.

I pace back and forth in the tiny stairwell landing, quickly reaching maximum agitation. Why is Deb saying this? When did she stop believing in us? When did she decide we couldn't overcome the odds?

"It's time to grow up, Danny," she says.

"Coming from the girl who is still doing what daddy says," I spit out. There's more venom in my voice than I've ever had with her. It isn't like me but I'm in free fall, not even knowing how literal that will be in just a few hours.

"I'm sorry," she whispers and gets quickly to her feet, running past me through the door, back towards prom.

I'm alone in the stairwell, the draft from the window raising goosebumps on my neck. I used to think the color painted over the concrete masonry in here was a warm tone of cream but it suddenly looks colder to me, a blue-toned white.

It's over. Everything is gone. Everything I have been working towards just fled out that door and I am empty, wrung out, and hollowed.

I walk out of the school without noticing or thinking about where I'm going. The teacher tasked with keeping us in the building until the end of the night must have gone to the bathroom; there's a half-drunk cup of punch on the floor next to the metal chair by the door.

The door slams shut behind me but I don't even hear it over the wind and the rain suddenly soaking through my clothes. What perfect weather for a night like this. I keep walking, letting my feet take me wherever they wanted to go.

I won't think about what happened next. I refuse.

Deborah

I push open the glass door of Cedar Harbor Hardware, the bell jingling overhead. My heart hammers in my chest as I ask the man behind the counter where I can find Danny. He gestures toward the back with a casual thumb, not looking up from his inventory sheet. I follow the narrow aisle past rows of hammers and paint cans, wondering if I'm making a terrible mistake coming here.

The day after the hockey game feels like a lifetime has passed. My muscles ache from the exertion, but it's my pride that's truly bruised. I'd made such a fool of myself—not on the ice, where I'd actually surprised myself with how well we played together, but afterward, when I'd reached for Danny's hand and suggested we give things another try. His face had closed off completely, and the pain in his eyes had shocked me into silence.

At the back of the store, a door stands slightly ajar, letting out the soft sounds of someone working. I hesitate, then peek through the gap. Sunlight streams through high, dusty windows, casting long rectangles across the concrete floor. And there's Danny, his back to me, bent over a cluttered workbench. He's working on what looks like a door hinge, his large hands moving with surprising delicacy as he measures something with a small caliper.

I don't announce myself right away. There's something mesmerizing about watching him work: the confidence in his movements, the way his shoulders flex beneath his flannel shirt, the absolute focus in his posture. This is Danny in his element, surrounded by the tools of his trade. Certificates hang in simple frames on the wall behind him. A pegboard displays an impressive array of tools, all organized with precision. Everything within arm's reach, I realize. Everything carefully placed for maximum efficiency.

He reaches for a wrench without looking, knowing exactly where it sits among the organized chaos of his workbench. I'm struck by how at home he seems, how solid and sure. This man bears little resemblance to the wounded boy I glimpsed yesterday when I clumsily suggested we could pick up where we left off three decades ago.

I clear my throat, suddenly aware I've been staring.

Danny turns his wheelchair, his expression shifting from concentration to surprise as he spots me hovering in the doorway.

"Deb," he says, his voice carefully neutral. "Didn't expect to see you today."

"I hope I'm not interrupting." I take a tentative step into his workspace, then another. "The guy up front said I could find you back here."

"Just finishing up a custom hinge for Mrs. Peterson's cabinet. Her cat somehow bent the original." His mouth quirks up slightly at one corner. "Animal weighs about twenty pounds. More of a small mountain lion than a house cat."

I laugh but we quickly fall into uncomfortable silence again. I shift my weight from one foot to another, feeling like I'm seventeen again, unsure what to do with my hands or where to look.

"About yesterday," I start.

"You don't have to—"

"Please," I interrupt, holding up a hand. "I came here to say something, and if I don't say it now, I might lose my nerve."

Danny sets down his tools and turns to face me fully, giving me his complete attention. Those eyes—they're exactly the same shade of warm brown they were in high school, but now they're guarded, cautious.

"I wanted to apologize," I say, the words rushing out before I can reconsider. "Not just for yesterday, but for ...before. For how things ended between us at prom."

He doesn't respond, just watches me with that steady gaze.

I take a deep breath. "What I did was cruel. Breaking up with you like that, in that stairwell—you deserved better. We'd been together for three years, and I ended it in the worst possible way."

"That was a long time ago, Deb." His voice is soft, but I can hear the old pain underneath.

"It was. But that doesn't make it right." I move closer, perching carefully on the edge of a metal stool near his workbench. "I've thought about that night so many times over the years. I've played it over in my head, wishing I'd handled it differently."

"We were kids," he says with a shrug that doesn't quite achieve the casualness he's aiming for.

"We were. And I was under a lot of pressure from my parents, from my community." I look down at my hands, twisting in my lap. "But that's not an excuse. I was a coward, Danny. I chose the easy path—what everyone expected of me—instead of standing up for what I felt."

His hands tighten on the seat of his wheelchair. "And what did you feel?"

The question hangs between us, loaded with three decades of unspoken history.

"I loved you," I admit quietly. "But I was scared. Scared of disappointing my parents, scared of being different, scared of the future. You were so brave, so sure of everything, and I...wasn't."

Danny is silent for a long moment, his eyes dropping to the metal parts scattered on his workbench. "I wasn't as brave as you thought," he finally says, his voice barely above a whisper.

"You were to me." I swallow against the tightness in my throat. "And I hurt you badly. I know saying sorry after all this time probably doesn't mean much, but I am sorry, Danny. Truly."

He looks up at me, his expression softening just slightly. "Thank you for saying that."

The workshop falls quiet except for the distant sounds of the hardware store—the bell over the door, murmured conversations, the creak of floorboards. Sunlight shifts as a cloud passes outside, briefly dimming the golden rectangles on the floor.

"There's something you should know," he says slowly. "Something I've never told you."

My heart beats a little faster at the seriousness in his tone. "What is it?"

Danny takes a deep breath, looking more vulnerable than I've seen him since we reconnected. "It's about that night. After prom. About how I ended up in this chair."

My chest tightens. As curious as I've been to know what happened, my mind is fighting against knowing that it's connected to that night.

Danny is completely still, looking down at the floor. "After you left me in that stairwell," he begins, his voice lower than before, "I walked out of the school. I didn't even notice how hard it was raining."

I nod, not trusting myself to speak.

"I just walked. No destination in mind. My tux was soaked through in minutes." He looks down at his legs, then back up at me. "I felt like everything was over. Like my entire future had just walked out that door with you."

My throat tightens. I want to interrupt, to apologize again, but something in his expression tells me he needs to get through this without interruption.

"I ended up at the train bridge overpass where we used to look at the stars." He pauses, eyes distant with memory. "I stood up there in the rain, looking down at the road. It was dark. Late. No cars. Just the rain on the asphalt, making everything shine under the streetlamp."

A terrible premonition begins to form in my mind. No, I think. Please, no.

"I wasn't thinking clearly," Danny continues, his voice steady but soft. "All I could see was you and Joel together, how perfect you'd look, how your lives would be everything mine could never be. I felt...worthless. Like I'd never be someone anyone could be proud to be with."

My eyes sting with tears I refuse to let fall. This isn't about my pain.

"You kept our relationship secret from your synagogue friends. I understood why, but it still hurt. You lied to your parents about me. You were ashamed of being with me." He shakes his head. "I don't blame you now. We were kids. But that night..."

He falls silent for a moment, and I can almost see him standing on that bridge, rain-soaked and heartbroken. The image is unbearable.

"I jumped, Deb."

The words land like physical blows. My hand flies to my mouth as a small, choked sound escapes me.

"Not my finest moment," Danny says with a humorless laugh. "I was seventeen, stupid, dramatic. I didn't realize that bridges that low don't kill people—they just break them."

I press my hand harder against my mouth, my entire body frozen with horror.

"Broke both legs in multiple places. Shattered my pelvis. Fractured my spine at L2 and L3." He recites the injuries like he's reading from a grocery list. "A trucker found me. I don't remember much after hitting the ground, just fragments. Lights. Voices. Pain."

"Danny," I whisper, his name barely making it past the knot in my throat.

"The doctors said I was lucky." His laugh is sharp, bitter. "The spinal cord damage was incomplete. That's why I have some function, can stand a little with support. Better than nothing, they said."

I can't stop the tears now. They slide down my cheeks as I imagine him in a hospital bed, broken and alone.

"My dad was devastated. Blamed himself. He worked two jobs to support us after my mom left, wasn't around much." Danny's eyes are dry, but his voice catches slightly. "He never knew about that night, about us breaking up. I told everyone I was drunk, lost control of my bike. Everyone thought it was an accident. I could never tell them I did it on purpose."

He meets my gaze directly. "No one in Cedar Harbor knows what really happened. Not Karen, not the guys on the team. No one."

Danny's hands move to the wheels of his chair, turning slightly back and forth—a nervous gesture. "It's not that I blame you. I don't. I made my choice that night. A stupid, impulsive choice that changed everything, but it was mine. I'm the one who climbed up there. I'm the one who jumped."

"But if I hadn't—"

"Stop." His voice is firm. "That's not why I'm telling you this. I'm telling you because what happened between us as teenagers hurt me very badly. More than you knew. And I spent years rebuilding myself, literally and figuratively."

He gestures around the workshop. "I went to trade school in this chair. Got laughed at, told I couldn't do the work. But I was determined to prove them wrong. Built this business from nothing. Made a life I'm proud of."

I think about the ladder at my cottage, the bungee cords, his confident movements on the roof. The evidence of his problem-solving was right in front of me all along.

"Every day was a challenge at first. Still is, sometimes. But I built this life, brick by brick, on my own terms." His eyes lock with mine. "I can't risk breaking like that again. I don't have it in me to rebuild myself a second time."

"I'm not the same person I was then."

"No? How do I know that? How do I know that you wouldn't take a better option as soon as it came along?"

I'm shocked how much his words sting. I want to push back and ask how he could think that of me but the truth is, he's not wrong. I keep saying I've changed but it hasn't been tested. He has no way to know if I'm no longer the kind of woman who would hide and downplay our relationship for the sake of appearances and discard him at the first opportunity.

So instead of arguing I nod. "I understand," I say. "I love you and I have loved you these past thirty-two years but I know that I haven't done anything to show you that and talk is cheap."

He says nothing, looks down at his lap where he's twisting his fingers.

"You should be proud," I say, meaning it with every fiber of my being. "What you've accomplished is incredible and I'm proud to count you as a friend."

He shrugs, uncomfortable with the praise. "It's just my life."

A silence falls between us, not exactly uncomfortable, but heavy with shared history and new understanding.

"No one else knows how you got hurt?" I ask again, still stunned by his confidence.

"No one." His eyes hold mine. "And I'd prefer to keep it that way."

"Of course." I wipe my tears, trying to compose myself. "I won't tell anyone, ever."

Danny nods, looking suddenly tired, as if the weight of his confession has drained him. "It was a long time ago, Deb. Another lifetime. I don't dwell on it anymore."

But I can see in the set of his shoulders, the tension in his jaw, that speaking about it has cost him. That some wounds, even those thirty-two years old, never fully heal.

"Thank you," I say finally. "For trusting me with the truth."

He looks at me for a long moment. "I needed you to know. Not to hurt you, but because..." He pauses, searching for the right words. "Because you deserved to understand why I can't just pick up where we left off."

"And I do. I understand." I hurt him more than I ever knew. I thought because he was a guy, he wouldn't care that I hid our relationship, that I acted ashamed of being with him. I never took his feelings into account. And all this time I've been letting myself believe that I did him a favor. I've pitied myself living in a marriage without love and thinking that Danny was out there living his dream life with everything he could ever want. I shielded and protected myself from seeing what a bitch I was to him.

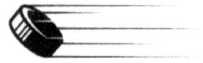

An hour later I'm standing in the middle of the old train bridge, my fingers tracing the rust-flecked railing as the late afternoon sun casts long shadows across the abandoned tracks. The metal is cold against my skin.

The bridge creaks beneath my feet as I take a tentative step forward. Below, the old county road stretches like a ribbon, empty except for a lone pickup truck disappearing around the bend. A crow calls from somewhere nearby, the sound stark against the stillness.

I close my eyes and try to imagine Danny here thirty years ago. It was raining that night. I remember worrying about my hair going flat. Did he stand where I'm standing now, hands gripping this same railing, before he...

I can't finish the thought. I open my eyes and look down at the pavement below. Not high enough to guarantee death, but high enough to break a body beyond repair. High enough to paralyze someone from the waist down. The realization hits me like a physical blow, and I have to grip the railing tighter to steady myself.

I'd broken up with Danny on prom night. I'd planned to wait until after—what kind of monster ruins prom?—but once we were there, slow-dancing under the spinning disco ball while Cyndi Lauper sang about time after time, I couldn't keep pretending.

"You'll break his heart either way," my mother had said, folding laundry with sharp, angry movements. "Better now than after you've wasted years."

So I did it. I broke Danny Wallace's heart.

I told myself it was for the best. That we'd both move on and find happiness elsewhere.

I never knew he'd come here afterward. Never knew he'd climbed this bridge in his rain-soaked tux and looked down at the road below and decided that a life without me in it wasn't worth living.

He said it wasn't my fault, that it was his own decision. But I was instrumental in making him feel unworthy. Everything I did to play it safe for my own life was making his life more and more difficult. I was too young and stupid to see how much I was harming him. I deserve to feel all the pain that's catching up with me now, and a whole new level of regret I didn't know was possible.

I press my palm flat against the rusted metal plaque that's still bolted to the railing. The date of the bridge's construction is barely legible beneath decades of graffiti—most of it faded now, but I can still make out a few names, declarations of love etched into metal and left to weather the years. Did Danny see these too? Did they make him feel even more alone?

Moss creeps along the edges of the concrete at my feet, reclaiming the man-made structure inch by inch. A freight train whistle sounds in the distance, the rumble carrying through the steel beneath my hands. The town hasn't changed much in thirty years. The same trains still pass through, the same families still gossip over fence lines, the same pressures still push young people toward paths chosen by others.

"I didn't know," I say aloud, as if Danny might somehow hear me across the decades. "I swear I didn't know."

But that's not entirely true, is it? I knew I hurt him. I just didn't care enough to check if he was okay. I was too busy reinventing myself at Harvard, too busy being Joel Klein's girlfriend and then his wife, too busy becoming the woman my parents wanted me to be. I left Danny behind without a backward glance, telling myself that first love always hurts but people move on.

Only he didn't move on. He stayed here, carrying the scars—visible and invisible—that I helped create. Building a life from the pieces left after his fall.

The wind picks up, sending a chill through my jacket. The sun is sinking lower now, the rose and gold streaks in the sky deepening to crimson. I should go, but my feet seem rooted to this spot. As if leaving means breaking some connection to the truth I'm finally facing.

When Danny pulled away from me in my cottage, when he said he couldn't risk trying again with me, I thought he was being stubborn. Holding a grudge. I never considered that his reluctance might be self-preservation of the most fundamental kind. Why would he trust me after what happened? Why would he believe I wouldn't walk away again?

A car passes beneath the bridge, headlights already on against the gathering dusk. Soon it will be too dark to see the road below. Too dark to stand here safely. I push back from the railing and take a deep breath.

"I'm sorry," I whisper, though there's no one to hear it. The words feel inadequate, but they're all I have. I can't undo the past. I can't change how I treated him then. All I can do is change how I treat him now. I can love him and care for him now even if he never accepts it and never lets me in again. And that's okay. Because love isn't about what you get back from someone else, it's giving with an open heart and not expecting anything back. It's showing kindness and respecting their boundaries, giving without asking to get.

I walk slowly back toward my car, each step feeling heavier than the last. The knowledge I carry now can't be unlearned. Can't be filed away neatly like the accounting problems I solve every day. This is messy and painful and demands something of me that I'm not sure I know how to give.

But as I drive away from the bridge, watching it grow smaller in my rearview mirror, I make a decision. I won't walk away this time. I won't take the easy path or listen to anyone else's idea of what my life should be. Whatever happens with Danny—whether he can forgive me or not, whether we find our way back to each other or not—I'm staying. I'm facing this.

Because thirty years ago, I chose what was easy instead of what was right.

I won't make that mistake again. Even if I lost my chance with Danny forever, going forward I know how to make the right choices.

Danny

The old screwdriver gives up with a crack that sounds too much like bone breaking. I stare at the sheared-off tip stuck in the stubborn hinge, my hands frozen in mid-air like I've been caught doing something wrong. The desk lamp flickers beside me, casting my shadow in uneven pulses across the cluttered folding workbench I've set up in the living room. Outside, dusk is falling, turning the windows into mirrors that show only my tired face and the mess I've made of what should have been a simple repair job.

"Piece of crap," I mutter, tossing the broken handle onto the workbench. It clatters against a pile of screws and washers. I rub my forehead where a headache is forming, a dull pressure behind my eyes that has nothing to do with the broken tool and everything to do with what I told Deb yesterday.

The truth. After thirty-two years of keeping it buried.

I wheel back from the workbench, needing space from the scattered pieces that suddenly feel too much like my insides—disassembled, exposed, impossible to put back together. The hinge can wait. Everything can wait. I've spent three decades waiting, what's a few more hours?

A car passes outside, headlights sweeping across my ceiling. For a second, they look like the fluorescent panels of the hospital, and I'm back there—an eighteen-year-old boy with a shattered body and a secret burning in his throat.

"You're lucky to be alive," the doctor had told my father, not me. Like I was a piece of furniture that had been salvaged from a fire. "The spinal damage could have been much worse."

My dad stood there in his work clothes, still smudged with grease from the garage where he'd been pulling a double shift when they called him. His face had gone gray, aged ten years in a single night. "But he'll walk again, right? Tell me he'll walk again."

The doctor's hesitation had been brief but unmistakable. "There's damage to the L2 and L3 vertebrae. The spinal cord injury is what we call incomplete, which means there's some function preserved. With extensive physical therapy, he may regain some mobility, but—"

"I'll do whatever it takes," I had interrupted, the first words I'd spoken since they brought me in. "I'll work harder than anyone's ever worked."

My father had squeezed my hand so hard it hurt, tears in his eyes as he nodded. "That's my boy."

And I did. I worked until my muscles screamed and my remaining nerves burned with effort. I clawed my way back to partial function, enough to stand briefly, to drag my feet forward with support. But never enough to walk normally again. Never enough to undo what I'd done to myself.

I never told him the truth. Not that night in the hospital, not during the endless months of rehab, not in all the years that followed until he died. He believed the story I made up—that I was out on my motorcycle in the rain, taking a corner too fast, losing control. An accident. Not a choice.

The community rallied around us. They held fundraisers for my medical bills, built the ramp at our house, delivered meals for months. Mrs. Simpson made a lasagna every Sunday for a year.

All for the poor Wallace boy. The tragedy. The accident.

Except it wasn't. And every casserole, every dollar, every kind word felt like another lie piling on top of the first one until I was buried beneath them all.

I wheel to the window and push it open, desperate for air that doesn't feel thick with the past. I breathe in the cold air, trying to clear my head, but the weight on my chest only seems to increase.

Telling Deb was like lancing a wound—painful, messy, but necessary. The relief I expected hasn't come yet. Instead, there's just this raw, exposed feeling, like I've ripped off a scab too soon and now I'm bleeding all over again.

What was I thinking? After all these years of keeping the truth locked away, why tell her now? Because she looked at me with those same eyes that once saw only the best in me? Because some part of me needed her to know exactly what she'd walked away from that night?

No, that's not fair. I didn't tell her to punish her. I told her because she deserved to know that she couldn't just waltz back into my life and pick up where we left off. That boy on the bridge died that night, and the man who emerged from the wreckage is someone else entirely. Someone who built his life on his own terms, without needing anyone's approval or love.

Or at least, that's what I've told myself.

My hands grip the wheels of my chair, feeling the treads on my palms. The familiar pressure grounds me, reminds me who I am now. Not the desperate teenager standing on that bridge in the rain, but a grown man who's faced his demons and survived.

But telling her has stirred something up, something I thought was long settled. All day I've been dropping things, losing my focus, my mind wandering back to the look on her face when I said those words: "I jumped, Deb."

The horror in her eyes, the tears. The way her hand flew to her mouth like she could somehow stop the truth from reaching her.

And now what? We're supposed to be friends? Teammates? How do you move forward after laying bare the worst moment of your life?

I close the window and turn my chair away, looking at the scattered tools and parts on my workbench. This is what I'm good at—fixing things, solving problems, making broken pieces work again. I understand the mechanics of hinges and doors, the physics of leverage and force. People are harder. Feelings are impossible.

But for the first time in decades, I wonder if maybe I'm tired of being alone with this weight. If maybe telling Deb was just the first step toward something I've been avoiding since that night on the bridge—forgiveness. Not from her, but from myself.

I wheel back to the workbench and pick up a pair of pliers. The broken tip of the screwdriver comes out of the hinge with a reluctant screech. I set it aside and reach for a new tool, something stronger this time. Something that won't break under pressure.

The lamp flickers again as I get back to work, my shadow jumping across the wall like it can't decide whether to stay or run.

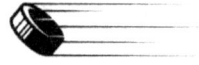

The door to Shop 3 groans as I push through, the familiar smell of sawdust and metal shavings greeting me like an old friend. Morning light slices through the dusty windows in sharp beams, illuminating the hanging tools and half-finished projects waiting for second period. I'm early, as usual, wanting to set up before the students arrive, but someone's beaten me here. Alana Klein perches against one of the lathes, her dark hair pulled back in a messy ponytail, those hazel eyes—so much like her father's—watching me with a mix of challenge and uncertainty.

"Morning," I say, trying to keep surprise from my voice. Students don't typically seek me out before class, especially not ones who've only been in town a few weeks. "You're here early."

Alana straightens up, hands tucked into the front pocket of her purple hoodie. "Yeah. I wanted to talk to you. Without everyone around."

That could mean trouble. I wheel over to my desk, setting down my bag of materials for today's lesson. "Everything okay with your project? The cutting board looked great last class."

"It's not about the project." She shifts her weight, suddenly looking younger than her seventeen years. "It's about my mom."

My hands go still on the desk. "What about her?"

Alana tilts her chin up in that defiant way teenagers have when they're nervous but determined. "You know, my mom has been happier than I've ever seen her since we came back here. I think you have something to do with that."

The directness catches me off guard. Like mother, like daughter—neither of them ones to beat around the bush. I busy myself arranging the day's materials, giving my face a moment to settle.

"Your mom and I are old friends," I say carefully. "It's nice to reconnect after so many years."

"That's the thing," Alana says, stepping closer to my desk. "I've never seen her like this before. She hums while she makes breakfast. She bought paint for the cottage without measuring the walls three times first. Yesterday she didn't even check if I'd done my trig homework."

I look up at her, surprised. "And that's...good?"

"It's weird. But yeah, it's good." She hops up to sit on the edge of a workbench, legs swinging slightly. "She was always so...I don't know. Controlled? With my dad, everything had to be perfect. The house, her clothes, me. It was like she was always walking on eggshells."

I nod, encouraging her to continue while I roll over to the supply cabinet, pulling out materials for the day's demonstration.

"Was she always like that?" Alana asks. "When you knew her before?"

I can't help but smile at the memory of teenage Deb, wild-haired and laughing as we raced our bikes down to the harbor. "No, not at all. Your mom was...spontaneous. Competitive. She'd challenge me to swim to the buoy and back even though she knew I'd always win."

"Mom? Swimming in open water?" Alana's eyes widen in disbelief. "She won't even go in past her knees at the beach."

"People change," I say, laying out wood samples on the demonstration table. "We were kids back then."

"But that's just it—she's changing back." Alana hops off the workbench, coming to help me with the supplies without being asked. "Ever since we moved here, it's like she's remembering who she used to be. And it started right after she ran into you."

I'm not sure what to say to that. The idea that I could have any effect on Deb's happiness after all these years seems impossible, yet here's her daughter telling me otherwise. And there's something about Alana—earnest beneath that teenage armor—that makes me want to be honest with her.

"Your mom and I were close once," I admit, lining up chisels on the workbench. "Best friends before we started dating. I always thought she could do anything she set her mind to."

"What happened?" Alana asks, quieter now. "Between you two?"

I choose my next words carefully. "Life happened. Different paths. She went to college, I stayed here."

"She married my dad," Alana fills in the blank.

"Yes."

Alana picks up a piece of sandpaper, running her fingers over its rough surface. "They were never right for each other. I think I always knew it, even when I was little."

"I'm sorry to hear that," I say, and I am—sorry that Deb spent years in a marriage that dimmed her light, sorry that Alana grew up watching her mother shrink herself. But there's a selfish part of me that wants to hear more, that wants confirmation that Joel Klein was exactly the wrong choice I always believed him to be.

"He's not a bad person," Alana says, as if reading my thoughts. "Just...rigid. Everything had to be his way, and Mom just went along with it. She turned herself inside out trying to be what he wanted."

I nod, keeping my face neutral even as I silently add another count to the list of reasons I'd like to introduce Joel's face to my fist.

"Were you guys serious? Back then?" Alana's looking at me with those eyes that miss nothing.

"We were young," I say, which isn't really an answer. "But yes, we cared about each other very much."

"And now?" She's watching me closely, this girl who looks so much like her mother did at her age.

"Now we're getting to know each other again. As friends." I meet her gaze steadily. "A lot has changed in thirty years."

Alana glances down at my wheelchair, then quickly back to my face. "Some things," she agrees. "But not everything. You still make her laugh. She hasn't laughed like that since...I can't even remember."

The thought of Deb laughing at something I said warms me in a way I don't want to examine too closely. "Your mother's a remarkable woman," I say instead. "Always was."

"She's scared," Alana says suddenly. "Of whatever's happening between you two. I can tell."

"So am I," I admit, surprising both of us with my honesty.

Alana studies me for a long moment, then nods like she's made a decision. "Well, I'm not scared. I think it would be good. For both of you."

Before I can respond, the bell rings and the sounds of students filling the hallway break the moment. Alana straightens up, slipping her teenage mask back on like armor.

"Don't tell her I said anything," she says quickly. "She'd freak."

"Your secret's safe with me."

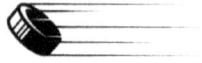

The pine-green paint catches the early afternoon light fil-
tering through The Whispering Pines' front windows. I
dip my brush carefully, tapping excess against the rim of
the can, and apply another stroke to the chipped banister.
The wood drinks the paint thirstily—these old houses are
always hungry for maintenance. I've been at it for nearly an
hour, but I'm making less progress than usual. My mind
keeps wandering, leaving my hands to do the work while
my thoughts chase themselves in circles, all of them leading
back to Deb.

I've already made three mistakes that I've had to fix—a
drip I didn't catch in time, a section where I painted over
dust instead of wiping it first, a spot where I pressed too
hard and left bristle marks in the wet surface. Rookie er-
rors. The kind I haven't made in years.

"Getting sloppy in your old age," I mutter to myself,
reaching for a rag to dab at a fresh mistake.

"Talking to yourself now? That's a bad sign."

I look up to find Karen standing at the bottom of the
stairs, clipboard in hand, watching me with a mixture of
amusement and concern. Her hair is escaping from the

bandana she's tied around her head, and there's a smudge of something that looks like flour on her cheek.

"Just keeping myself company," I say, turning back to the banister. "How's the booking situation looking?"

"Full through Valentine's Day," she says, tapping her pen against the clipboard. "You know, for someone who's been painting that same section for twenty minutes, you don't seem to be making much progress."

I glance down at the banister, surprised to find she's right. I've been going over the same foot-long stretch again and again, barely noticing.

"Sorry," I say, dipping my brush again. "I'll pick up the pace."

Instead of moving on, Karen sets her clipboard down and lowers herself to sit on the bottom step, just beside where my wheelchair is positioned. She's close enough that I can smell the lavender soap she always uses.

"You seem distracted," she says, not a question but an invitation.

I keep painting, focusing on the smooth pull of the brush through wet paint. "Got a lot on my mind."

"Anything to do with a certain newly divorced accountant?"

My brush hesitates, leaving a small bubble in the paint that I quickly smooth out. "Maybe."

Karen waits, knowing me well enough to recognize when I'm gathering my thoughts. We've been friends for over two decades, ever since she hired me to renovate the B&B's front porch. She's one of the few people who's never treated me with kid gloves, never acted like my disability was the most interesting thing about me.

I stop what I'm doing and close my eyes briefly. "I take a lot of physical risks but—"

"You haven't taken an emotional risk in years?" she finishes for me.

"Yeah." I turn to look at her, finding only understanding in her face. "How'd you know?"

"Danny, I've watched you climb ladders no sane person would attempt, fix roofs in thunderstorms, and once hang upside down from my gutters to install a bird feeder. But I've never seen you let anyone get close to you. Not in all the years I've known you."

I dip my brush again, more to have something to do with my hands than because the banister needs another coat. "It's different."

"Is it?" She tilts her head, studying me. "Or is it just scarier?"

"Both." I apply paint in a careful stroke, watching the way it transforms the wood from faded to vibrant. "Physical stuff...if I fall, I hurt myself. I can handle that. But with people..."

"You might hurt someone else," she supplies. "Or they might hurt you."

I nod, grateful that she understands without me having to find the words.

"But you're tempted now?" she asks gently.

"Exactly." I set down the brush, turning my chair slightly to face her more directly. "Seeing Deb again, after all these years...it brings everything back. The good and the bad."

"And you're wondering if it's worth it." Karen's eyes are kind but direct. "If she's worth it."

"Is it?" I ask, the question that's been eating at me since I told Deb the truth about my injury. "Worth the risk?"

Karen is silent for a moment, considering. "You know I met Susan when I was forty-seven," she says finally. "After my divorce, I swore I'd never put myself through that again. Too painful, too messy."

I nod, remembering how closed-off Karen had been back then, throwing herself into renovating the B&B instead of dating.

"Then this annoying, persistent woman came along," she continues with a small smile, "and no matter how many walls I put up, she just kept finding ways around them. And I had to decide—was protecting myself worth missing out on something that could be wonderful?"

"Obviously you decided it wasn't," I say.

"I decided that fear is a lousy compass," Karen corrects. "It'll keep you safe, but it'll also keep you small."

I absorb this, looking down at my paint-speckled hands. "It's not that simple. Deb and I...there's history. Complicated history."

"There always is," Karen says with a shrug. "That's what makes it real."

"And there's this," I add, gesturing to my wheelchair. "I'm not the guy she knew back then."

Karen's expression sharpens. "You think that matters to her?"

"I don't know," I admit. "It would to some people."

"If it matters to her, then she's not worth your time anyway," Karen says bluntly. "But I don't think it does."

"How can you be so sure?"

"Because I've seen the way she looks at you," Karen says simply. "Like she's found something she thought was lost forever."

The words hit me with unexpected force. I turn back to the banister, needing something solid to focus on.

"Look," Karen continues, softer now, "I'm not saying jump in with both feet. I'm just saying...maybe it's time to consider that some risks are worth taking. That protecting yourself from pain also means protecting yourself from joy."

"And if it all goes wrong?" I ask, voicing the fear that's been gnawing at me.

"Then you'll handle it," she says with absolute confidence. "Like you've handled everything else life has thrown at you. But at least you'll know you tried."

I pick up my brush again, letting her words sink in. Karen stands, retrieving her clipboard from the floor.

"For what it's worth," she adds, "I think you two make sense together. I've been running this B&B for twenty years. I know chemistry when I see it."

With that, she leaves me to my painting and my thoughts, the sound of her footsteps fading down the hallway. I look at the half-finished banister, the green paint gleaming wet in the afternoon light. It will dry eventually, transformed into something new but still fundamentally the same underneath.

I dip my brush and continue working, each stroke more deliberate than the last. Maybe Karen's right. Maybe some risks are worth taking, even with all the uncertainty they bring. Maybe especially because of that uncertainty.

Deborah

I sit at my parents' formal dining table, trapped in the gleaming prison of bone china plates and crystal glasses that catch the light in fractured rainbows. The silver has been polished to a mirror shine, and the white tablecloth is so pristine it hurts my eyes. My mother has brought out the good napkins, the ones with the hand-embroidered edges that we only use for special occasions. This should have been my first clue that tonight wasn't just a casual family dinner, but I was too distracted by work and Alana's college applications to notice the warning signs. Now I'm stuck here with Joel sitting beside me, close enough that our elbows almost touch when I reach for my water glass, while my parents beam at us from across the table like they've just orchestrated the social coup of the century.

"More asparagus, Joel?" My mother offers the silver serving dish with the eagerness of a gift-bearer, her diamond tennis bracelet catching the light as she extends her arm.

"Thank you, Esther," Joel says, his voice carrying that same measured tone he uses with difficult patients. He takes a modest portion, always careful about portions, always counting calories and noting serving sizes. "The meal is wonderful, as always."

"We're just so happy you could join us tonight," my mother says, her eyes flicking to me with meaning so thick I could spread it on toast. "It's been too long since we've all been together like this."

My father clears his throat in that particular way that means he's about to say something he thinks is casual but is actually calculated. "Joel was telling me about his practice earlier. Did you know he's expanding to a second location in Brookline?"

"No," I say, pushing a perfectly roasted baby potato around my plate. "I didn't."

"Very prestigious area," my father continues. "And he just hired two new associates. Graduates from Harvard Medical."

I take a sip of wine, larger than is probably appropriate for my mother's crystal stemware. Joel shifts in his chair beside me, his knees bumping the table slightly.

"It's nothing, really," he says with practiced humility. "Just keeping up with patient demand."

"Nothing?" My mother's voice rises with pride. "You're being modest. A thriving medical practice is something to be proud of. And in this economy!"

I stab a green pea with more force than necessary. When my mother called to invite me to dinner, she'd said nothing about Joel being here. "Just a family dinner, dear. We haven't seen you in weeks." I should have been suspicious when she suggested Alana go to a friend's house instead. Should have known they wouldn't just let me be.

"Debbie," my mother says, using the childhood nickname I've asked her not to use for twenty years, "Joel was telling us how he's been thinking about buying a vacation property. Something on the water, maybe."

Joel clears his throat. "I've been looking at places on Cape Cod. Nothing fancy, just a little three-bedroom near the beach." He turns toward me, his eyes searching mine with an expression I've seen hundreds of times before—a mixture of hope and wariness. "It would be good for Alana, having a place to go in the summers. She always loved the beach as a little girl."

"She still does," I say automatically, then instantly regret giving him this opening.

"See?" My mother pounces. "Alana needs that kind of stability. A familiar place to go, family traditions. That's what children thrive on."

I twist my napkin in my lap, winding it tighter and tighter around my fingers. My chest feels too small for my lungs.

"And let's be practical," my father adds, setting down his fork with the precise movement that signals he's about to deliver what he considers sage wisdom. "Financial security is nothing to dismiss, Deborah. Especially at this stage of your life. You're not getting any younger, and real estate is one of the few reliable investments these days."

Joel's fingers drum lightly on the tablecloth beside his plate. I can practically feel the nervous energy coming off him in waves.

"Dad, I have a good job," I say, trying to keep my voice even. "I'm doing fine financially."

"Of course you are, dear," my mother says in that tone that means she doesn't believe me at all. "But there's doing fine, and then there's doing well. You've always been independent, but there's nothing wrong with accepting help when it's offered from someone who cares about you."

Joel's hand moves to the pocket of his sport coat, and I feel a cold knot form in my stomach. He withdraws a small black velvet box, setting it on the table between our plates with trembling fingers.

"I wasn't planning to do this quite so...formally," he says, a flush creeping up his neck. "But since we're all here..." He doesn't open the box, just lets it sit there like a bomb waiting to detonate. "Deborah, I know things weren't perfect between us. I know I made mistakes. But these past few months, seeing you with Alana, talking more often about her future...I've been thinking that maybe we could give things another try."

The room seems to shrink, the walls pressing in. I stare at the little black box, my mouth suddenly dry. This isn't happening. This can't be happening. Not when I've finally found myself again. Not when I've finally reconnected with Danny.

Danny. The thought of him sends a flutter through my chest, completely different from the tightness I feel now. Danny with his quiet strength, his self-deprecating humor, his hands that build and fix and hold with such care. Danny who knows who I really am, who's seen me at my worst and still looks at me like I'm something precious.

"Joel, I—" I start, but my mother cuts me off.

"Just think about it, dear. That's all anyone's asking." Her smile is wide but her eyes are sharp. "Joel's been very patient, very understanding about this...phase you've been going through."

Phase. Like moving back to Massachusetts, finding my own place, rebuilding my life on my terms is some kind of temporary madness I'll soon recover from.

"Your mother's right," my father chimes in. "No need to decide anything tonight. Just consider what Joel is offering. For Alana's sake, if nothing else."

I push another pea around my plate, watching its small green body leave a trail through the sauce. Joel's fingers twitch toward the box, but he doesn't touch it again. Instead, his hand hovers near mine on the table, not quite making contact. Waiting for permission, as he always does now. As if proper etiquette can make up for the years of subtle control, of quiet dismissals, of my opinions being considered but never quite valued.

I twist the napkin tighter in my lap, feeling the fabric strain against my fingers. How easy it would be to slip back into the comfortable rhythm of my old life. The security, the respectability, the known quantity of being Joel Klein's wife. My parents would be ecstatic. Alana would have her father close again. Everything would be...fine.

Fine, but never joyful. Fine, but never free. Fine, but never truly mine.

I look at the velvet box sitting between our plates, at Joel's hopeful face, at my parents' expectant smiles, and something inside me begins to crack—not with weakness, but with the pressure of truth demanding to be released.

The air in the dining room seems to thicken, becoming harder to breathe as my mother places her cool, dry hand on my forearm. Her grip is gentle but insistent, like her voice when she leans closer and whispers, "Think about what's best for Alana, dear." The words are familiar—how many times has she used my daughter as the ultimate trump card? As if Alana's happiness and my own are somehow separate things, as if one must be sacrificed for the other. I look down at my mother's perfectly manicured nails against my skin and feel something tighten in my chest.

"Joel has always been good to you both," my father adds, his voice carrying that particular blend of affection and authority he's perfected over the years. He dabs his mouth with his napkin, a gesture that somehow manages to look definitive. "Even through the divorce, he's been generous. That counts for something, Debbie."

Joel clears his throat, seeming to take courage from my father's endorsement. "I know we had our differences," he says, his voice softening into the tone he uses when he's trying to sound vulnerable—a trick I once found endearing but now recognize as calculated. "But I think we can make it work this time. We're older, wiser."

My mother nods enthusiastically, as if Joel is reciting poetry instead of vague platitudes.

"I've already looked at a few properties," Joel continues, warming to his subject. "There's a place in Chatham with a private beach access. Three bedrooms, a sunroom facing the water. We could spend weekends there, holidays. Alana could bring friends in the summer." His eyes take on that dreamy quality they get when he's envisioning something perfect. "It could be a fresh start for all of us."

I glance around the dining room, my eyes catching on the family portraits that line the walls. My parents on their 40th anniversary, posed in formal wear. My high school graduation, with Joel standing proudly beside me. Our wedding photo. Alana's baby pictures. Joel and me on either side of her at her bat mitzvah. A documentation of the perfect family narrative my parents have always cherished. The weight of expectation in those frames is almost physical, pressing down on my shoulders.

"I've given this a lot of thought, Deborah," he says, using my full name the way he does when he's being serious. "I know I wasn't always present during our marriage. The practice demanded so much time, and I... I took you for granted. I see that now."

My mother adds, "People make mistakes, dear. The question is whether you learn from them."

I think about Danny. About his honesty in telling me what happened after prom night. About the way he rebuilt his life without bitterness or self-pity. About how he makes me laugh, how he sees me—really sees me—not as an extension of himself or a project to perfect, but as I am. I think about the cottage, my cottage, with its crooked shutters and worn floors that I'm fixing bit by bit, on my terms. I think about the woman I've become since moving back to Cedar Harbor, and the one I'm still becoming.

"The thing is," Joel says, misreading my silence as consideration, "we already know each other's flaws. There won't be any surprises this time. And we both want what's best for Alana. She'll be off to college soon, but she'll still need a stable home to come back to. Parents who are united."

United. The word strikes me as wrong somehow. Joel and I were never truly united, even when we shared a house and a bed. We occupied the same spaces, followed the same schedules, but we were always separate, our cores untouched by each other. Not like with Danny, where even a simple conversation feels like a meeting of true selves.

"I miss our family," Joel says, his voice dropping lower, intimate. "I miss you."

His fingers finally make contact with mine, the touch light but proprietary, as if he's already staked his claim. Something inside me—some long-suppressed spark of rebellion, of self-preservation, of truth—suddenly flares hot and bright. The sensation is so strong, so visceral, that I almost gasp.

Without planning it, I'm on my feet. My chair scrapes loudly against the hardwood floor, the sound breaking through the careful civility of the dinner table. Three startled faces look up at me.

"Dad, Mom," I say, my voice steadier than I expect, "I love you for caring. I love that you want what's best for me and Alana. But Joel isn't the one I need."

My mother's mouth opens in shock, but I press on before she can interrupt. "I tried that path. For thirty years, I tried to be the daughter you wanted, the wife Joel wanted, the mother Alana needed. I twisted myself into shapes that weren't mine, and it nearly broke me."

Joel's face has gone very still, his eyes wide and unblinking.

"The truth is," I continue, my heart pounding but my voice strong, "Danny is the one. He always was. He has my whole heart, my whole chest. He sees me for exactly who

I am, and he doesn't try to change me or mold me into something more convenient."

The silence in the dining room is absolute. My mother's face has lost all color except for two bright spots of red high on her cheeks. My father sits frozen, fork suspended halfway to his mouth.

"If he can't forgive me for the past, so be it. That's my burden to bear. But I won't settle for less than real love ever again. Not for financial security, not for appearances, not even for what you think is best for Alana."

I straighten my shoulders, standing taller than I have in years. The napkin falls from my fingers to the floor, a small act of liberation.

Joel's expression is carefully controlled, but I can see the muscle twitching in his jaw—a sure sign of suppressed anger.

"I'm sorry," I say, meaning it. "I should have been honest sooner. With all of you. But especially with myself."

I pick up my water glass and take a sip, surprised to find my hand isn't shaking. The stunned silence stretches across the table like a physical thing, but for the first time in this house, the silence doesn't make me anxious. It feels like power. Like truth.

"Alana deserves to see her mother happy," I say finally. "Really happy. Not just going through the motions of a convenient life. That's what I want her to learn—to choose joy over obligation, every time."

My mother recovers first, her spine straightening as if someone's pulled an invisible string attached to the top of her head. She exchanges a quick glance with my father before turning back to me with a carefully composed expression. "Deborah, sweetheart," she says, her voice gentle like she's talking to a child who's just had a tantrum, "I understand you're going through a lot of changes right now. Divorce is emotionally confusing, and it's normal to...revisit old feelings." She reaches for my hand, which I've pulled back to my side. "But making decisions based on nostalgia isn't wise."

"Your mother's right," my father adds, setting down his fork with a precise click against the fine china. "You need to think clearly about this. Danny Wallace was a high school romance. You're remembering the good parts and forgetting why you chose to move on in the first place."

I notice how they say his name—Danny Wallace—like it's a diagnosis, a condition I need to recover from.

Joel himself hasn't spoken. He sits very still, his profile sharp in the dining room's overhead light. With deliberate movements, he closes the velvet box that still sits on the table and tucks it back into his pocket. His face is a careful mask, but I know him well enough to see the wounded pride in the tightening around his eyes, the slight flush creeping up his neck.

"He was your first love, dear. That's always powerful," my mother continues, her voice taking on that reasonable tone she uses when she thinks she's being the adult in the room. "But you're not seventeen anymore. You have responsibilities, a reputation in the community."

My father leans forward, elbows on the table despite my mother's rule against it. "And let's be practical for a moment. You're talking about a man who's..." He hesitates, searching for a word that won't sound unkind. "Limited. Physically limited. Have you really thought about what that means? For your future? For Alana?"

Something cold slips down my spine. "This has nothing to do with him, really. This is about me. He's already rejected me, which I can hardly blame him for. But that doesn't mean I slip right back to a life that wasn't working. Whether Danny Wallace every takes me back or not, I am done with what other people want me to be."

Joel clears his throat, finally finding his voice. "I never meant to make you feel that way," he says, and there's genuine regret in his tone. "I thought I was helping."

"I know," I tell him, softer now. "That's what makes it so sad. We were never right for each other, Joel. Not really. We were just...convenient. For our parents, for the community, for our own expectations of what life was supposed to look like."

My mother makes a small, distressed sound. "You're being unfair. Joel has always—"

"Been good to me. Yes, I know." I reach for my purse hanging on the back of the chair. "And he'll make someone a wonderful husband someday. Just not me."

I can see my father preparing another argument, the one about financial security and stability that he's been making since I was old enough to understand what money meant. But I've heard everything he has to say a million times already.

I gather my keys from the small table in the entryway where I'd left them hours ago, when I still thought this was just a family dinner. Joel stands too, his movements stiff with dignity.

"Thank you," I tell him, meaning it. "For being a good father to Alana. For trying. I want you to know that I'll never stand between you and her. She needs you in her life."

He nods, his expression softening slightly. "And I'll always be there for her." He hesitates, then adds, "For both of you, if you need anything."

"I appreciate that."

I step outside into the cool evening air, pulling the door closed behind me with a soft click that feels somehow momentous. The night wraps around me, dark and vast and full of possibility. My heart pounds in my chest—partly from fear, partly from exhilaration—as I walk to my car. I've just burned a bridge that's stood for decades, rejected the safe harbor my parents have always offered.

But as I slide behind the wheel, hands trembling slightly as I insert the key, I feel something else rising beneath the fear—a fierce, wild joy. For the first time since I was seventeen, standing in that high school stairwell making the wrong choice, I feel fully, completely alive. Whatever happens next—whether Danny can forgive the past or not—I've finally chosen my own path.

The engine turns over, and I pull away from my parents' perfectly manicured lawn, heading back toward the crooked little cottage with its worn floors and pink shutters.

Danny

I wheel myself into the back of Steamy Beans just as Kathleen is adjusting the microphone stand for open mic night. I didn't plan to come tonight—these kinds of gatherings usually make me feel like I'm taking up too much space—but Karen mentioned something about "good local talent" with a look that made me suspicious. Now I scan the crowd, wondering what she's up to, while positioning my chair against the wall where I can see everything without being seen.

The place is packed tonight. String lights crisscross the ceiling like constellations, casting a warm glow that softens the edges of everything. I recognize most of the faces—the regulars from the hardware store, a few of my students' parents, some of the guys from the hockey team. Murph catches my eye from across the room and raises his coffee mug in greeting. I nod back, settling into my spot as Kathleen taps the microphone.

"Welcome to another Open Mic Thursday at Steamy Beans," she says, her voice carrying through the speakers with a slight crackle. "We've got a great lineup tonight. Please hold your applause until after each performance."

I reach for the cup of black coffee I ordered on my way in. It's still hot enough to warm my hands through the paper sleeve. A young girl with blue hair steps up to the mic first, reading a poem about climate change that has too many metaphors but plenty of heart. The crowd snaps their fingers appreciatively when she finishes. Next is an older man with a guitar who plays a folk song I vaguely recognize, his weathered fingers moving with surprising grace across the strings.

I'm not really paying attention. I keep wondering why Karen was so insistent I come tonight. She knows I don't like crowds much, prefer the quiet of my workshop or the isolated peace of a rooftop repair. Yet she'd practically pushed me out the door, telling me I'd regret missing it. I'm about to text her to ask what the hell she's up to when Kathleen steps back to the microphone.

"Next up is someone new to our open mic night," she says, her eyes scanning the room until they land on me with a knowing look that makes my stomach tighten. "Please welcome Deborah Klein."

My coffee cup freezes halfway to my mouth. I set it down carefully, suddenly aware of how my hands might betray me by shaking. Because there she is, walking toward the microphone with that determined stride I remember so well, chin up despite the nervous flutter of her hands. She's wearing jeans and a simple blue sweater that brings out the green in her eyes, her hair falling in waves around her shoulders. She looks beautiful. She looks terrified.

I sink deeper into my corner, grateful for the shadows. Does she know I'm here? I search her face for any sign, but her eyes are fixed on the microphone as she adjusts it with unsteady fingers. The café has gone quiet, that particular hush that falls when something unexpected is about to happen.

And then she starts to sing.

I recognize the opening notes immediately—"Forever Young" by Alphaville. Our song. The one that was playing the first time I kissed her at Allie Mckenzie's party in junior year. The one we slow-danced to at every school dance for two years. The one that was supposed to play at prom right before everything fell apart.

Her voice is soft, untrained but sweet, carrying the melody with a vulnerability that makes my chest ache. She makes it through the first verse before stopping abruptly, her hand coming up to her throat.

"I'm sorry," she says with a self-deprecating laugh that ripples through the room. "I'm not here to entertain you. I'm actually here to make a fool of myself for love."

A murmur runs through the crowd. I sit perfectly still, hardly breathing.

"Thirty-two years ago, I made the biggest mistake of my life," she continues, her voice steadying. "I chose what was safe and expected over what was real and true. I let fear guide me instead of love." She takes a deep breath. "Danny Wallace might not forgive me, and that's his right. But I need him to know that I'm not afraid anymore and I'm not hiding my feelings anymore."

My heart is hammering so hard against my ribs I'm sure the people nearest me must hear it. The café has gone completely silent.

"I choose him," she says, her voice clear and certain. "Like I should have done thirty years ago and I'm saying it publicly because he never should have had to feel like I was hiding him or ashamed of him." Her fingers twist together in front of her. "I choose the man who rebuilt his life with incredible strength and courage. Who teaches kids to create beautiful things with their hands. Who fixes what's broken with patience and care." Her voice catches. "Who deserves someone brave enough to love him without reservation or fear. All of you here know Danny. I'm willing to bet that all of you here have been helped by him. He deserves to know that every person who has him in their life is lucky beyond words. I don't say this with any expectation or hope. I say this because I made him feel small and I need to make up for that. Thank you, everyone."

A woman near the front—I think it's Carly—lets out a little "aww" that seems to break the tension. Suddenly there are nods, smiles, a few scattered claps. Sam reaches over to squeeze Robbie's hand, their heads tilting together. Murph is grinning into his coffee like he's known all along this was coming.

My throat feels tight, something hot and unsteady building behind my eyes. I press my palms against the wheels of my chair to ground myself, to stop the trembling that's started in my fingers. Deborah hasn't seen me yet. She's fumbling her way off the stage, her face bright red, looking at the floor. She can't get far because there's too many people around her.

I'm in a state of shock. It feels like the café has transformed around me, though it's the same people, the same lights, the same smells...everything is different. My entire body feels strange, hollow and full at the same time, like I might float away if I loosen my grip on my chair. Because everything I've told myself for thirty-two years—that she never really loved me, that I wasn't enough, that I'd been right to keep my walls up—is crumbling in the face of her raw honesty.

A shift ripples through the café, like water disturbed by a stone. Heads turn in my direction, expressions changing from appreciation to expectation. Kathleen's eyes find me in my corner, and her smile spreads slow and knowing across her face. I feel the attention like a physical thing, pressing against my skin, pushing me out of the shadows. Deborah is still standing to the side of the microphone, confused by the sudden change in the room's energy, until Murph deliberately turns in his seat to look my way. Her eyes follow his movement and then she sees me.

For a moment, everything stops: the murmurs of the crowd, the ticking of the clock above the counter, maybe even my heart. Her face goes still with recognition, color draining and then rushing back. The microphone picks up her sharp intake of breath, a sound so small and yet so loud in the sudden quiet.

"Danny," she says, barely audible even with the mic. She doesn't move, frozen in place like she's afraid I might disappear if she blinks.

I don't know what my face is doing. I've spent decades perfecting the art of keeping my thoughts hidden, of presenting a calm exterior while chaos reigns inside. But whatever she sees there gives her the courage to continue. She straightens her shoulders, her gaze never leaving mine.

"I don't expect anything," she says, her voice steadier now. "I just needed to stop hiding the truth."

The café is still silent, a held breath of collective anticipation. I feel the weight of every eye in the room, all these people waiting to see what I'll do. Waiting to see if thirty years of hurt can be undone by courage and truth.

I push my chair forward, the movement breaking the spell of stillness. The crowd parts without a word, creating a clear path between us. Murph touches my shoulder briefly as I pass, a silent gesture of support. I keep my eyes on Deborah's face, watching as uncertainty and hope battle across her features.

The distance seems both endless and too short. Each foot of wooden floor brings me closer to a decision I never thought I'd have to make. My hands are steady on my wheels, each movement deliberate. When I reach her, I stop, looking up at her tear-streaked face.

"Danny, I—" she starts, but her voice catches.

"You sang our song," I say, the words coming out rougher than I intended, scraped raw by emotion.

She nods, wiping quickly at her cheek. "Not very well."

"Better than I remember," I tell her, feeling the corner of my mouth lift in spite of everything.

The café around us has become a backdrop, the people mere shadows at the edge of my awareness. There's only Deb, standing tall but trembling slightly, her courage more evident in this moment than even on the hockey rink.

"Thirty years is a long time to wait for an apology," I say, my voice gentler now. "But I think I'm done waiting."

Her eyes widen, uncertain of my meaning. "I didn't do this to force you or anything, I just had to—"

I reach up and take her hand, cutting off her words. Her skin is soft against my callused palm, familiar and strange all at once. I tug gently, pulling her down toward me. She understands immediately, kneeling beside my chair so our faces are level, her eyes searching mine.

"I was eighteen and stupid," I tell her, quiet enough that only she can hear. "I made a terrible choice that night. But looking at you now..." I pause, finding the right words, the true ones. "Maybe we both needed to become who we are before we could find our way back to each other."

Her hand trembles in mine. "And who are we now?" she asks.

"People who've learned the hard way what matters," I answer. I reach out with my free hand, letting my palm cup her cheek, feeling the dampness of tears against my skin. "People who know what they want."

And then I'm kissing her, or she's kissing me—it doesn't matter which. Her lips are soft against mine, hesitant at first, then more certain. My hand moves from her cheek to tangle in her hair, pulling her closer as the kiss deepens, becoming more than a tentative question—becoming an answer.

Someone in the crowd whistles. Another person claps. Suddenly the café is erupting in cheers and applause, the sound washing over us like a wave. I feel myself smile against her lips, my shoulders relaxing in a way they haven't in decades. The weight I've been carrying, all that old pain, doesn't disappear, but it shifts, becomes lighter somehow.

We break apart, foreheads touching, both breathing a little harder than normal. The café continues its celebration around us, but we're in our own space, our own moment.

"What now?" she whispers, her eyes searching mine.

"Now we start over," I tell her. "Not from where we left off. From here. From who we are now."

Her hands tighten on my shoulders. "I'd like that."

I lean in closer, my lips near her ear to murmur something only she can hear: "Besides, I still need to teach you how to score a proper goal without falling on your ass."

Her laugh bursts out, bright and surprised, breaking through the last of her tears. She presses her forehead against mine again, shoulders shaking with laughter and relief. "You're never going to let me forget that, are you?"

"Not a chance," I say, grinning. "I've got thirty years of giving you a hard time to make up for."

Her expression turns serious again, though her eyes still shine. "I've got thirty years of loving you to make up for too."

It's such a Deb thing to say—honest and direct, no hedging or hiding. I feel something tight in my chest finally release, a knot I've been carrying so long I'd forgotten it was there. I take her hand and press it against my heart, let her feel its steady beat under her palm.

"We've got time," I tell her.

The End

Thank you for reading! If you enjoyed this book I hope that you'll consider **leaving a review** wherever you purchased this book and/or Goodreads. It helps a lot :)

You can get **bonus scenes,** short stories, character art, and more at my website: https://ruthmadisonbooks.com/bonusincluding spicy scenes for all Cedar Harbor titles and "Wheelchair Mafia" merch.

www.ingramcontent.com/pod-product-compliance
Lightning Source LLC
Chambersburg PA
CBHW070104260626
47160CB00004B/1317